"So I must love my enemies . . . "

"I have listened to you, my Maggie. I have become a shame to my family, a coward to my enemies. To please you, I have avoided making my enemies pay for slaying my brother, and, no longer afraid of us, they dare to invade and kill our women and children.

"Enough of your peace talk, enough of your Christian ways. It is *our* way that will be followed from now on." He thrust her away from him with a force that sent her reeling until she collapsed on the floor.

How ironic, that in the moment when he renounced her and her ways that he had never before spoken the English language so fluently.

WHERE MORNING DAWNS

Irene Brand

Serenade/Saga
BOOKS
of the Zondervan Publishing House
Grand Rapids, Michigan

A Note From The Author:
I love to hear from my readers! You may correspond with me by writing:

Irene Brand
1415 Lake Drive, S.E.
Grand Rapids, MI 49506

WHERE MORNING DAWNS
Copyright © 1986 by Irene Brand

Serenade/Saga is an imprint of Zondervan Publishing House, 1415 Lake Drive, S.E., Grand Rapids, Michigan 49506.

ISBN 0-310-47522-8

Printed in the United States of America

86 87 88 89 90 91 92 / 10 9 8 7 6 5 4 3 2 1

PREFACE

In 1584 Sir Walter Raleigh obtained permission from Queen Elizabeth I to explore and colonize eastern North America. In that year Raleigh's representatives explored the Atlantic Coast, taking possession of the land for England, naming it Virginia in honor of Elizabeth, the Virgin Queen.

The following year Raleigh sent out another expedition to establish a settlement and build a fort on Roanoke Island off the coast of present-day North Carolina. Friction eventually developed between the colonists and the native population, and when food supplies ran low, the Englishmen left America.

Raleigh decided to try again, and in 1587 a party of 115 colonists, including seventeen women, nine children, and two native Americans, sailed to Virginia under the command of John White. In a few weeks, White found it necessary to return to England, and three years later, when he returned to the New World, the colonists had disappeared. Although many legends have surfaced about the fate of those colonists, little evidence has been authenticated about their disappearance and history continues to refer to that colonizing attempt as "The Lost Colony."

Margaret Lawrence, Towaye*, Richard Shabedge, Thomas Topan, Jane Pierce, and the Prats were all listed as members of the 1587 expedition, but no other information is available about them. Their origin and destiny are part of that great mystery of the colonization period.

Where Morning Dawns is a fictitious story of what may have happened to Raleigh's colonists.

*Pronounced *tau-ī*.

CHAPTER 1

EARLY MORNING MIST shrouded the small ship as it left the turbulent Atlantic waters, nosed its way slowly through the narrow inlet and entered the placid sound. Maggie Lawrence strained her eyes to see from her position on the main deck what lay before them. As the boat turned northward, sunlight burst through the haze to spotlight the wooded area a short distance away. Roanoke Island!

Turning to her friend, Jane Pierce, who stood beside her, Maggie said, "Look at the sunlight, Jane! God is giving us a sign of His continued presence with us. We've reached the land where morning dawns."

"Aye," Jane replied, holding securely to the hand of her nephew, John Prat, who was straining for freedom so that he might play with the other children on the pinnace. "Let's pray it's also a land where our dreams will come true."

"Oh, it will be," Maggie returned with confidence. "After weeks of confinement on that ship, my only dream is to have my own home again—one that won't toss and turn—a place to provide for my family," Jane said. "My dreams aren't great ones like yours."

A soft sea breeze, flavored with salty spray, enveloped them, and Maggie threw back her hood, loosing rebellious flaxen hair to be ruffled by the breeze. With the edge of the hood she wiped moisture from her face, knowing that the dampness wasn't caused entirely by the boat's spray. Tears dimmed her blue eyes as she savored the significance of this hour, and momentarily she lost sight of Roanoke Island with its sandy beaches and gently rolling hills. She was entering a new world in more ways than one. Soon to be married to Richard Shabedge, she tried to envision the life of mission they would share as they spread their faith to the natives of Virginia.

"I still can't believe Father and Mother allowed me to join Raleigh's colonists. But," she said, flashing a smile at her older friend, "I suppose with you and Uncle Thomas to look after me, they thought I'd be safe enough."

Jane, a widowed sister of Roger Prat, had joined the colonists to look after Roger's son. Close neighbors in Devon, Maggie had known Jane all of her life, and took comfort from her presence.

"Yes, and your father is a firm believer in following the dictates of one's own conscience. Since he and Mr. Shabedge broke with the Church of England to establish our small band of dissenters, he could hardly deny you the same privilege of choice, especially when you insisted God was calling you to bring the gospel to this land." Jane gave Maggie a squeeze. "I haven't forgotten who you always imitated in your child's play."

Maggie laughed as she remembered. "Queen Isabella, of course! I always envied that great woman who did so much to bring Christianity to this newly-discovered land. It's been almost one hundred years since she sent the first missionaries here. The English are late arrivals."

She reached out idly and tried to touch the white sea bird that had settled on the sail rope near them, but the bird flitted away with a startled squawk.

John had at last broken loose from his aunt's grasp and was racing toward the forecastle of the boat, and as Maggie glanced that way, she saw the alert figure of a man who stood there. One foot resting on a water cask, a firm hand grasping the rigging of the sails, he gazed ahead intently. *Towaye!* Thus he had stood for hours on their journey across the Atlantic. Although a zeal had burned within her heart to evangelize among the American natives, Towaye was the first one Maggie had seen. Captured by a former British expedition to America, he was now returning to his homeland as an interpreter for the English.

Perhaps conscious of her gaze, Towaye turned, fixed her with a keen-eyed survey, and momentarily their glances held until Maggie looked away. Maggie and Towaye had not exchanged words during the ocean voyage, but the few glances they had shared had been more meaningful than conversation.

The gentle rise and fall of the pinnace was suddenly broken when the small vessel struck a sandbar, and the travelers were forced to continue their journey to the island in a four-oared wherry. Since many of the male colonists had been on the island several days preparing dwellings for their families, most of the pinnace's passengers were women and children. Still, two trips in the wherry were required to get everyone to land, and Maggie took the last.

She gathered up her long skirts and jumped from the boat toward the sandy beach, but the many weeks at sea had made her legs wobbly. A strong hand grasped her arm and steadied her. Surprised, Maggie looked up into the face of Towaye, at close range for the first time. During the months he'd spent in England, Towaye had adopted European dress; thus, only his brown skin and slightly slanted eyes seemed alien.

A tight gray doublet revealed his muscular arms and back, and the knee-length breeches above long stockings fit loosely over lean hips. Maggie lost awareness of the other colonists as his dark eyes held her spellbound, and a gentle smile played around his lips. "Welcome to my homeland," he said, for her ears alone.

Maggie was surprised at the ease with which he spoke English. She gently removed her arm from his grasp, and said, "Thank you, Towaye. I trust we will be welcomed by all your countrymen."

"You will always be welcome in my village," he said, and his black eyes gleamed with intensity. With a little nod, Maggie moved away from him and dropped to her knees on the sand. As she bowed her head she became conscious of the sounds around her. Children raced along the beach, splashing in the water, releasing the energy stored up on the ocean voyage. Some women wept quietly, while men busied themselves lifting supplies and household items from the boat.

"God, we thank You for the safe journey," Maggie began her prayer, but when she thought of their unsettled future, and the problems confronting them, she thought, *How can I pray?* Abandonment on this island when they had intended to settle on the more fertile, larger Chesapeake area two days farther north had discouraged them all.

"Dear God," Maggie continued her petition, "even if our plans have gone awry, I commend my future to You. I still remember the divine calling I received to spread the story of Jesus to the natives here." In her mind Maggie seemed to hear Jesus say, "When you

10

go into all the world, I'll be with you," and she rose, comforted.

To her right she noticed Towaye leaping into the air, waving his arms toward the sky, and muttering unintelligible words. Suddenly he threw a handful of green leaves into the water, and fell to his knees, his eyes closed, his face turned upward to the heavens.

Some sort of strange religious rites, Maggie surmised. *Richard and I have a great challenge before us.*

Most of the other colonists had disappeared, Maggie noted, but she saw Thomas Topan, her uncle, accompanied by Richard Shabedge, her betrothed, making their way toward her along the beach.

Richard was thirty years old, ten years Maggie's senior, and they shared, if not a great love, the same burning missionary zeal. Thus they were betrothed with the blessing of her parents, and they now awaited the approval of Richard's father, who had been in America for over a year, before they married.

The dampness had turned Maggie's hair into a mass of ringlets, and she covered her head as she turned to greet first her uncle, and then Richard. Thomas patted her on the shoulder, and Richard tenderly squeezed the hand she held out to him.

"We're sorry we weren't here to greet you, but we were delayed at a meeting of the colony's leaders," Thomas said. "But your home is ready, such as it is."

Thomas led the way, and Maggie and Richard followed along the sloping trail through the woods. They soon entered a small village surrounded by loblolly pines, oaks, dogwoods, and cedars. Her uncle stopped before a building covered with a thatched roof. Maggie experienced a hint of homesickness as she entered the low door, reminded of the farmers' cottages in Devon, England.

The cottage was of simple construction, with four

corner posts curved and joined overhead to form a Gothic arch at each end. The frame was joined by tie-beams, and at intervals down the side walls vertical posts were filled with split laths and sealed with mud and plaster.

"This dwelling isn't very commodious," Thomas apologized, "but in such a short time, we couldn't manage anything else."

Maggie was appalled when she compared this barren room to her father's stone manor in Devon. At one end of the cabin was a large open fireplace, backed with brick, and with a chimney of timber and daub. A few crude chairs stood around a table made from a giant log. One open window allowed light to seep into the otherwise gloomy room.

Thomas opened a small door to the left of the fireplace. "This will be your room, Maggie. It will afford you a bit of privacy."

Maggie peered into the room where the trunk containing her belongings had been thrown on the earthen floor beside a wooden bedstead built into the wall. The few coverlets she'd brought from England were on the bed, giving the room some semblance of home.

"I wish I had a better report for you, Maggie, but the success of our venture is doubtful," Thomas told her as they ate the gruel he had prepared. "This island is too small to support our large group, and the Indians Governor White expected to help us have fled. Their village is deserted—not one native is left on the island."

"You mean no Indians have been here at all?"

Thomas and Richard exchanged glances, and Maggie caught her breath as Richard shrugged his shoulders. "We might as well tell you. One of our men was killed several days ago by natives, and in retaliation Governor White led an attack on a mainland village. I fear these events will hamper our efforts to evangelize the natives."

Maggie dropped her wooden spoon into the bowl in front of her. "What dreadful news! From all reports, I thought we could expect a welcome from the Indians."

"We may have been given a distorted view of conditions here just to entice us to join Raleigh's colonists," Thomas said.

"Yes, the natives are distrustful of Englishmen now," Richard added, "and not without some reason."

"But surely in a year your father has been able to achieve some kind of peace with the natives, Richard?" Alarmed by the significant silence, Maggie cried, "Your father, Richard! Where is your father?"

Richard's face had blanched, and his brown eyes above the neatly shaped beard were full of concern. "We've no word of him, nor the other Englishmen left here last year. One skeleton was found when we landed, but I am sure it wasn't my father. Governor White did learn from a few friendly natives on another island that our men left Roanoke in the midst of an Indian attack, but that's all we know."

"So you see, Maggie," Thomas said, "your plans to be married will have to be postponed. Without Mr. Shabedge, there's no other preacher among the colonists except Richard, and he can't very well marry himself." Thomas smiled a wry smile.

Maggie lowered her head to avoid Richard's eyes. Was it relief she felt that she wouldn't be married right away? That was a foolish thought. Of course she wanted to marry Richard. Without the pending marriage her parents would never have allowed her to come on this journey. Yet she would have liked a more emotional relationship with the man she married. Richard was a good man, and he would be kind to her, but inwardly she longed for a loving companionship such as she had witnessed between her mother and father. *But I'm marrying Richard as a part of my duty to God.* That should be enough, but in her heart she knew it wasn't.

Lifting her eyes, hoping her relief wasn't mirrored there, Maggie said, "We can wait, Richard. With the other changes we've had to accept, we can't start our Indian mission anyway. What are your immediate plans?"

"Towaye is leaving for his town, Winnetoon, in the morning and I'm going with him. That will give me an opportunity to survey the land, as well as to ask questions about my father and the others who are lost. I'm hoping I can find news of Father in one of the Indian villages along the way."

A storm had raged for three days—rain and strong winds battering the forlorn residents of Roanoke Island, but today the sun was shining, and Maggie started her day's work with more enthusiasm than she'd felt since their arrival on the island. She had endured a constant battle with the fireplace in an effort to prepare the meals, and even it seemed to cooperate today. In Devon she had often watched the cook prepare the family's meals, but that experience had hardly equipped her to cook over this open fire, and with only a few utensils. The fireplace had smoked during the stormy days, and Maggie opened the door to allow fresh air to cleanse the cabin. She was stirring stew in the only iron pot she possessed, inhaling its zesty scent, when Jane Pierce appeared in the doorway.

Maggie pushed curling tendrils of hair away from her flushed face, and greeted Jane. To escape the heat of the cabin, they sat on the brick steps. Fortunately the previous expedition to the island had made some bricks, because the colonists hadn't found any stones for building purposes.

"Is it true that Richard plans to return to England with Governor White when he leaves in a few days?" Jane asked at once.

Maggie stared out through the forest to where a flash of blue water was visible, wondering how the two large ships that had brought them to Virginia, now anchored off shore, had fared in the storm. If they had been damaged, Richard might not be leaving after all.

"Yes, he thinks he should take the news of his father's disappearance to his mother. Then, too, he wants to collect some more supplies. He believes we should build our mission further inland, rather than here along the coast. He thinks the natives in Towaye's region are more friendly than the ones in this area."

Jane nodded her graying head. "They probably haven't endured the aggravation from the explorers that these coastland Indians have."

Noticing Thomas coming into the clearing from the woodland, Maggie lifted her hand in greeting. Towaye stalked behind him, and Maggie became uncomfortable as she looked at the younger man.

Jane laughed lightly, and said, "What do you think of his attire?"

Upon his return to Winnetoon, Towaye had reverted to his native dress, and he was as nearly naked as any man Maggie had ever seen. Unclothed except for a fringed deerskin apronlike skirt that hung a few inches below his thighs, he carried a bow, and a quiver of arrows was slung over his shoulders. His head was shaven except for a black roach of hair down the center of the head from front to back. Towering a foot over Thomas, his slender body was firm and muscular.

"Dinner won't be ready for a while yet," Maggie said quickly in an effort to hide the confusion she experienced at seeing so much physical perfection. Towaye might have been a bronze statue sculpted at the hands of Michelangelo.

Nodding to Jane, Thomas answered, "No hurry, Maggie. Towaye has shot a deer. He will bring it in, and teach you how to prepare the meat."

"Fine," Maggie agreed with a quick glance at Towaye. He was looking at her, and she turned back to Thomas. "The storm has washed many shells up on the beach, and the children have been gathering them. I want to look for a few to send to my parents. Do you think it's safe for me to go alone?"

Thomas stroked his pointed gray beard. "I'd rather you didn't, Maggie. If hostile Indians will strike once, they may try again. I'd go with you, but I must be at a meeting this morning to make plans for the future of the colony while Governor White is gone." He turned to Towaye. "Would you go with Mistress Lawrence to look for shells?"

Towaye gravely nodded and started toward the beach motioning for Maggie to follow.

"Why not go with us, Jane?" Maggie invited as she picked up a basket.

"No, thank you," Jane declined. "I must see what John is doing. That boy can find more mischievous things to do." She shook her head in fond dismay.

Maggie tried to catch up with Towaye, but each time she reached his side, he would put forth a burst of speed and precede her again. Finally she caught his arm, and said, "Stop running away from me. I want to talk to you, and I can't talk to your back all the time."

He gave her a reproachful glance. "Woman walks behind man. It is our way."

Maggie clutched his arm until his steps slowed. "It isn't *our* way, so slow down. I want you to teach me your language. If we're going to live here, I must learn to speak to the people. Will it be difficult for me to learn?"

"I will teach you, my Maggie," he said as they left the forest and came to the edge of the water. Maggie started at his easy use of her given name, but she supposed that was *his way,* too.

Maggie's head barely reached his shoulder, and she had to look upward to his face.

"Are you happy to be in your own country again?" she asked, and watched the transformation of his usually somber face as he smiled.

"Yes, my Maggie," he said. "Here I am free. In England, I was a slave. Hated that, hated the noise, the smell of the people, and the cities, too."

"How did you have the opportunity to return with us? Did you run away?"

"Governor White want me. Thought I could be of help to colony."

"You speak English well to have been in England such a short time." They were wading through sea weeds reaching to Maggie's waist, and when they rounded a small cove, the beach before them was littered with brightly colored shells. Towaye stooped to pick up a shell, and handed the colorful item to Maggie, who placed it in the basket. The soft lapping of the surf sounded peaceful to Maggie after the stormy weather of the past few days.

"Knew English before. A white man lives in Winnetoon, our town."

"An Englishman?" Maggie asked in surprise.

He nodded his head. "Peter Colman. You know, my Maggie?"

"No, I don't think so. But how and why did he arrive there?"

"Stayed behind two-three seasons ago when the first English came. He likes our town and ways."

17

Maggie spent the next half-hour choosing a variety of shells, thinking of her mother's pleasure at receiving this gift from the New World. Although her basket was full, Maggie picked up one more shell, washed the sand from it, and held it to her breast. It would make a pretty ornament. Towaye reached for it. "I fix necklace for you."

Since she had more than enough shells to send to England, Maggie relinquished that one to his waiting hands, and her pulse quickened when their hands touched. She tried to keep in mind that Towaye was a savage, a heathen, an unlearned native who had no part in her life except as a person to be converted to the Christian faith. But when he looked at her with those piercing black eyes and called her, "My Maggie," she had trouble remembering anything except that he was a man and she was a woman.

The fragile shells had been packed carefully between several layers of leaves into a woven basket Towaye had provided. Surely they would be safe from damage on the voyage to England. Now Maggie was writing a letter to her parents for Richard to deliver along with the shells.

Few women of her generation could read and write, and Maggie was thankful once again that her father hadn't looked with disfavor upon an educated woman. Her brothers had gone to school, and had eagerly shared their knowledge with her, and when tutors had visited the manor house, Maggie had had lessons, too. Her book knowledge would stand her in good stead for the teaching she hoped to do on this continent.

City of Raleigh
The 25 August, 1587

My dear parents,

Greetings from your dutiful daughter, Margaret. The ocean voyage was rigorous, and our welcome in Virginia much different from what we had expected, yet we thank God for bringing us thither. Despite the bickering of our officials, and a delay in the Caribbean while the ship's captain looked for Spanish vessels to plunder, we reached the coast of North America in mid-July. Upon our arrival at Roanoke Island, the ship's captain refused to take us on to Chesapeake, only two days' sail northward.

Other surprises awaited. The earthen fort built a year ago by Englishmen had been torn down, and although the houses were still standing, it was obvious they hadn't been inhabited for a long time. The nearby Indian village was also deserted, and no news had yet been received of the Englishmen, including Mr. Shabedge, who had been left here the preceding year.

A few days before our arrival one of the colonists was killed by hostile Indians, which has caused some fear amongst us. Many of the natives seem unfriendly now. Richard is considering some adjustments in our plans.

Not all the news is bad, however. Two weeks ago we had a very impressive ceremony when Richard baptized Manteo, one of the native Americans who sailed with us, and named him Lord of Roanoke under instructions from Sir Walter Raleigh. The following week, Eleanor Dare's daughter, Virginia, was born, giving Governor White his first grandchild, and just this morning, another of our colonists gave birth to a child. Thus life goes on.

Uncle Thomas sends his greetings, and promises he will take good care of me. Do not worry about us. Despite the uncertainties of our future, I'm happy to be doing the will of our Father in heaven, into whose care I commend you.

> *Respectfully,*
> *Maggie*

No tears came, but Maggie had a large lump in her throat. This letter to her parents seemed even more final than her leavetaking from Plymouth three months before. Maggie refused to believe, however, that she wouldn't see her family again. The elder Lawrences planned to someday emigrate to this new land in search of religious tolerance.

Maggie checked the venison stew simmering over the slow-burning fire, and hurried to change her clothes before Thomas and Richard came. Because of the crowded conditions on board ship, and the efforts to cope with a modified life style, Maggie hadn't bothered with her bulky farthingale for months. But tonight she attached the hoop, causing her blue linen dress, a shade lighter than her eyes, to stand out from her slim hips. Carefully brushing her hair, she piled it on her head, adding an illusion of height to her slight figure. On his last evening with her before he sailed, Maggie wanted to give Richard some pleasant memories to take with him.

Voices in the other room announced the arrival of her menfolk, and Maggie went to greet them. Richard's eyes lighted at sight of her, and he surreptitiously squeezed her hand when Thomas turned his back to place his harquebus on the wooden plank above the fireplace.

"How did the meeting go?" Maggie asked.

"Not too good, I'm afraid," Thomas answered. "Let's eat first, and we'll tell you about it. What smells so good?"

The two men pulled the rough chairs close to the table, and Maggie lit the whale oil lamp before she spooned the stew into some wooden bowls, and served them Yorkshire pudding that she had baked in a Dutch oven under the coals.

"It's venison stew. I added some native vegetables that Towaye brought me. He assured me that they were safe to eat, so I'm trusting that he knows."

Richard gave her a look almost like a warning. "You can trust him, and I only hope he stays here with the colonists instead of going back to Winnetoon. If you need any help, go to him."

He spoke the words so emphatically that she wondered if Richard was worried about their survival. She had been concerned only with the fact that he faced two sea voyages before they could be reunited—the thought hadn't occurred that she might not be here to greet him when he returned.

Conversation was limited during the meal, although Richard complimented Maggie on the food. She was gratified to note that the Yorkshire pudding tasted good in spite of all the substitutions she'd made in the ingredients. When their appetite was sated, Richard and Thomas turned to the affairs of the City of Raleigh.

"I suppose there's nothing else White can do but go back to England, but I wish he wouldn't," Thomas said. "That will leave Ananias Dare as our leader. I like the man, and he seems the logical one to be in charge because he's Governor White's son-in-law, but I'm not sure he's capable of making major decisions."

Thoughts of home had been flooding Maggie's mind all day. Thus she could sympathize with Governor White, who would be leaving his family behind in America.

"Doesn't he mind leaving his new grandchild?"

"Probably," Richard said absentmindedly as he arranged the ruff around his neck. Maggie realized that he, too, had dressed more carefully for their final evening together.

Thomas, perhaps sensing the desire of the betrothed couple to be alone, made an excuse to leave them. As his footsteps faded, Richard took Maggie's right hand and touched the narrow gold ring on her third finger. From around his neck he drew a gold chain to which a similar ring was attached.

"Do you remember our betrothal ceremony, Maggie?"

That service when she and Richard had knelt before their small band of believers was still vivid in Maggie's mind. Their leader had separated the triple ring, giving one circlet to her; Richard was given one section; and her father had received the third one, which he had later entrusted to Thomas Topan. It now rested in a box on the mantle, and on her wedding day, Maggie would receive the other two pieces to join with her own.

"Yes, I do," Maggie answered. "I remember the preacher said the vows we had taken were as binding as our marriage pledges would be, and could be broken only by death, or by mutual consent."

Richard caressed her hand, but she was insensitive to his touch. "I hope you won't be sorry you made the vows, my dear. I must confess I hesitate to leave you here with so many unmarried, eligible men, but I trust you, Maggie."

"Those vows are as sacred to me as the ones I took to serve God here in this country. You *can* trust me," Maggie said impulsively.

When Thomas's voice through the half-closed door signaled his return, Richard bent, and for the first time, placed a hasty kiss on Maggie's lips. "I wish you were going with me so we could be married sooner," he said.

"I will wait for you, Richard. What does another year matter when we have a lifetime before us?"

CHAPTER 2

THE NEXT MORNING Maggie stood with Richard on the beach and listened to the water surging gently against the sand. The mementoes Governor White would carry to England were loaded into a small boat for transport, with the passengers, to the large sailing ships off the coast. Maggie looked thankfully at the pinnace anchored nearby. They would have at least one ocean-worthy vessel left at Roanoke Island.

When the governor appeared with his family, Richard bent and quickly kissed Maggie's cheek. "Surely I can return within six months, Maggie. Stay true to me. Even though it's delayed, we can still be married and carry out our mission here. The natives need to hear the gospel, and we'll teach them of Christ and His ways."

Maggie longed to say, "Don't go, Richard," for she feared the long separation and her doubt that their marriage would ever become a reality. A year could pass before Richard's return to Virginia, and Maggie knew she might face starvation if the colonists couldn't learn to live off the land. The supplies they'd brought wouldn't last indefinitely. Surrounded as they were by unfriendly natives, Maggie wondered if her chances for survival were as good as Richard's.

Lost in reverie as she watched the small boat leave the sound for the rougher waters of the Atlantic, Maggie started when an arm circled her waist. Jane Pierce stood beside her.

"Thanks for thinking of me, Jane. I'm feeling very lonely and afraid."

"Don't be concerned, Maggie. I'm sure all will be well with us. God has promised to be with us everywhere. Remember Jesus said, 'I'll go with you to the end of the world.' "

Maggie laughed softly. "And it seems we've just about reached the end of the world." She glanced around, seeing that the other colonists had returned to their houses, and said, "Let's walk along the beach. We won't need to start cooking yet."

The sand was wet, and their pointed, flat-soled leather shoes left imprints on the beach. They picked their way through debris that had been washed ashore by the recent storm. Maggie removed her hood, and the sea breeze filtered through her hair, seeming to free her from the doubts that had plagued her. She skipped along the water's edge, and reaching a quiet cove, sat down on the sand, removed her shoes, and dangled her feet in the cold water.

"Maggie," Jane spoke a word of warning. "Do you think it's wise for us to be here by ourselves? Remember the Indians killed one of our men. While those who killed him have apparently disappeared, they could return. Let's go back to the settlement."

Maggie reluctantly put on her shoes and started to retrace their journey, but she smiled when Towaye stepped out of the forest and followed them. No need for concern when he was on guard, so she continued to dawdle along the beach.

With Towaye by her side, Maggie knew she need not fear wandering into the forests, learning what foods to gather. Wild grapes grew in abundance along the beach, and he helped her gather them into baskets, showing her how to dry them for winter's use. The days passed rapidly as she learned the ways of the forest. Once they discovered an Indian boat washed up on the beach, and Towaye pulled it into a small creek, and fastened it securely.

"May need someday," he said.

He turned and handed her the pink shell she had uncovered several days before. A neat hole had been drilled into the edge, and a plaited chain of vines was inserted through the hole.

"Thank you, Towaye. You're very good to me. It's pretty." Pleased, Maggie dropped the necklace over her head and admired it.

"But not as pretty as you, my Maggie." She felt her face flushing as she looked at him in surprise. "Maggie," he continued, "a nice name, but not my name for you."

In spite of her embarrassment, Maggie smiled at him, and asked, "What name would you use?"

"Golden Hair. Do you know, my Maggie, that your hair glistens like the gold in the hills and the rivers? I found my gold in you."

Who would have thought this pagan American had the soul of a poet? His comment alarmed her, and she hurried down the beach away from him, but he soon overtook her, placing his hand on her arm.

"Don't be angry with me, my Maggie. Don't leave me."

Maggie trembled at his touch, refusing to look at him, and because her thoughts were confused, she became angry.

"Don't call me your Maggie! If you're going to live among the English you need to learn our customs.

25

You should call me 'Mistress Lawrence,' and be more formal when you talk to me. I'm betrothed to Richard Shabedge, and we're going to be married when he returns—live together as man and wife."

"Richard is a good man, but not the man for you. I want you."

Stung by the boldness of his words, she moved away from him. "Don't ever say that to me again. You're always talking about *your* way. Well, it isn't 'our way,' for a man to say such things to a woman. Do you understand?"

Maggie couldn't interpret the expression in his eyes, and she turned her back on him to walk quickly away. When she was several yards down the beach, his words reached her.

"Very pretty when you're angry, Golden Hair."

Maggie whirled to face him, amazed to see a glint of sardonic amusement in his eyes. Englishmen could talk about the native Americans being innocent and childlike if they wanted to, but Maggie would never believe it again. Not for one moment had Towaye believed she meant what she had said. He had looked into the depths of her soul and correctly reasoned that she wasn't nearly as angry as she should have been.

Maggie avoided Towaye for several days until another incident occupied her mind. Peter Colman, the Englishman who'd been living among Towaye's people, came to Roanoke Island for a visit, and his appearance created quite a stir. Colman was dressed in deerskin shirt and breeches, and his hair and beard hadn't been trimmed for many months. The colonists, eager to gain firsthand knowledge of one who'd existed in the American wilderness, converged on the Dare home to hear of Colman's experiences.

"I came with the first expedition under Amandas and Barlow in '84." Colman explained. "I liked the country, and when the others headed back to England, I disappeared into the forest. For several months I wandered from one village to another, and I was treated well enough, but at last I arrived at Winnetoon, and there I've stayed. I've found the Algonquian tribes to be friendly.''

Ananias Dare spoke after Colman had explained his presence in Virginia. ''What are our chances for survival and safety here?'' Maggie's heart skipped a beat when Colman's face darkened, and he shook his head discouragingly.

''Many of the tribes in this area are angry about the return of the English. They've suffered at the hands of the earlier expeditions, and I figure you'll be attacked within a short time. Then, on this island, you hardly have enough room to sustain a large group of people. How many of you are here?''

''More than a hundred,'' Thomas Topan said, ''and each family has been promised five hundred acres of land by the promoters of the colony.''

''This is no place for you,'' Colman said shaking his head emphatically.

''We know that,'' Dare answered, ''but our captain refused to take us to Chesapeake where we were planning to settle.''

''Why not move on your own?'' Colman counseled. ''There's some good land on the north side of the Chowan River just a few days' journey from here, and the Chespian Indians are peaceful now. Even though that pinnace is small, you could move everyone in two trips, and now is the time to go before winter hits this area.''

Immediately the colonists divided themselves—those who wanted to follow Colman's advice, and those who said they must remain in Roanoke until White's return.

Maggie's own future was in waiting for Richard's

return, but she had no voice in the matter, and she trembled at the final agreement. Those who wanted to leave the island outvoted the others. The largest number of colonists would move to the Chowan River area, while a small group remained on Roanoke to await White's return. Lots were cast to decide which colonists would go or stay, and Thomas' draw made him one of the men to remain on Roanoke.

"Maggie," Thomas said as soon as they were alone. "I want you to go with the others. I don't like the idea of your staying here with so few people to protect you, and I'm responsible to your parents for your welfare."

"With your permission, Uncle, I prefer to stay. There will be some weaponry left for our protection, and I'll probably be just as safe as I would be with the others. They'll be open to attack on their journey, and shelters will have to be built when they arrive at their destination. With winter coming, their prospects aren't good either."

Thomas squeezed her around the shoulders, as near as her bachelor uncle had ever come to affection. "I'm drawn between two opinions, Maggie. Your company is pleasant, and I like to know firsthand how you're faring. But there's safety in numbers, and I think the natives will hesitate to attack the large force. However, the decision is up to you."

"I'll stay," Maggie said.

"So be it. Trust God it's for the best."

Within a month the larger band of colonists was gone. Maggie held her tears until she bid goodbye to Jane Pierce. "Don't cry, dear," Jane said, even through her own tears. "It won't be long until you join us. Trust God. If it was His will for us to come here, He will care for us."

Maggie trusted God, but not even Richard's departure had caused the desolation she felt as she watched the heavily laden pinnace disappear slowly from sight. She was marooned on an island with her uncle, twelve other white men, and Towaye.

Peter Colman went north with the rest of the colonists, indicating his intention to return to Winnetoon when he saw the group safely settled, but Towaye seemed to have no thought of leaving. He shadowed Maggie's footsteps, sitting on the steps when she arose in the morning, never out of her sight unless she was inside her house.

But what would they have done without him? He taught the men to hunt with bows and arrows, enabling them to keep their meager supply of gun powder. He helped them cut deer meat into strips and showed them how to dry it for storage. He went with Maggie into the forest to gather the tubers to be put into stews, persimmons to be made into pudding, and nuts and acorns to be added to their stores. Maggie learned from Towaye that they could be ground into powder to be used in bread making. Already Maggie was hoarding their scanty reserve of grain, but the more she saved it the smaller the supply seemed to grow.

One pleasant, sunny day when Maggie thought they'd laid in all the supplies they needed, she asked Towaye to take her on a tour of the island. She had become accustomed to seeing the deer herds grazing throughout the forest, but was startled when, on their walk, they came upon a herd of goats.

"How did those get here?" she asked, looking at the animals in amazement.

"English bring, I think."

"But not this time!" Maggie said. "We didn't have room for livestock."

"Important, Maggie? Do they go wild in English woods?"

Maggie was delighted to see the horned, strikingly beautiful white and black goats similar to the large herd on her father's farm. "No, they're domesticated animals."

"Domesticated?" Towaye stumbled over the strange word.

"We have them in our fields and barns. They are useful to us." Maggie strove for words to explain their use of domestic animals. "We milk them—use their milk for food."

"Good to eat?" he asked, fingering the arrows in his quiver.

Maggie grabbed his hand. "Yes, but don't you kill any of them. They're more valuable to us for their products. Help me drive them back to the fort." But the dozen or so animals scattered at their approach, and Maggie had to forget capturing them for the time being.

"We'll get some help and take them to the village," she said, but Towaye looked doubtful.

Not long after losing sight of the herd of goats, they entered the small clearing of a deserted Indian village.

"Home of Roanoke tribe," Towaye explained.

Maggie peered with interest at the houses that were built of cedar, surrounded by a circle of poles driven into the ground. The village had only one entrance and the spiked poles would have made climbing over the palisade impossible.

"Is this like your village?" Maggie asked.

"A little, but we don't have the wall. Winnetoon bigger, too."

The houses were barren of any furnishings, and Maggie asked, "Why did they leave, do you think?"

"Afraid of English, probably, but tribes move around a lot. Not unusual."

When they were ready to leave the village, Maggie heard a familiar clucking, and glancing behind one of the huts, she saw a brown Dorking hen scratching in the soil to find food for eight chicks.

"Why, I can't believe this!" she cried. "If I didn't know better, I'd think I was back on my father's farm in Devon. Let's catch them, Towaye; I want to take them back to the village."

"To eat?"

Did he assess everything for its food value? she wondered. "We *can* eat them, but not until there are lots more. Help me." She cautiously walked toward the hen which clucked imperiously to the chicks until they ran under the protection of their mother's feathers.

"Now if we just had something to throw over them, we could catch them all at once." She looked around, but with Towaye's skimpy clothing, he could certainly spare nothing, so she quickly lifted her skirt and unfastened one of her underskirts. With one brisk movement she ripped the garment until it formed a flat cloth.

Towaye watched her, and his expression suggested that he thought she'd lost her wits.

"When I throw this over them, you help me gather them up into the cloth. They won't like it, but we can carry them back to the settlement this way. Move quickly."

Towaye did as he was bidden, and they soon had the squawking hen and all but one of her cheeping offspring imprisoned in the skirt. Maggie took the bundle from Towaye's grasp.

"Please catch the little one, Towaye," she said. Catching the chick took a great deal of effort on his part, and he looked as if his male dignity had been offended to waste so much time on a miniature fowl. When Maggie opened the bundle a bit for him to slip the chick inside, the hen pecked his finger. Muttering angrily, he withdrew his hand, and patted the knife at his belt significantly.

"Don't you dare!" Maggie said. "This is the beginning of my flock of chickens—a little bit of England transferred to Virginia. Just wait until you eat pudding thickened with eggs, and you won't be so angry."

The commotion caused by the outraged hen made conversation impossible as they walked back to the settlement, and Towaye looked affronted.

Maggie laughed delightfully. "This is *our* way, Towaye."

Whatever his feelings, Towaye helped Maggie build a small enclosure to house her flock. Thomas Topan came home as they finished their work. "Grenville's expedition brought a lot of livestock with them," Thomas said, "and these are probably remnants of that time. He brought horses and cattle, as well, and I'd like to know what happened to them."

After two days of cold rain, Maggie walked to the doorstep and breathed in the fragrance of a blue autumn morning. Hazy white clouds chased each other across an aquamarine sky.

Towaye was waiting for her, a spear in hand. "Going fishing this morning. Bring a big basket."

The possibility of some fresh fish overrode her irritation at his commanding tone. She walked beside Towaye to a secluded area of the shore, where he stopped, and began stamping his feet, clapping his hands, and alternately holding up his arms and staring into the heavens. Even though Maggie was learning some of his language, she couldn't understand the strange words he voiced. With one final leap into the air, he scattered several handfuls of crushed leaves into the water.

"Now why did you do that?" she asked.

"Offering tobacco to god of the sea to bring the fishes."

Maggie stamped her foot in annoyance. "That's foolishness."

"You'll see, my Maggie. Catch lots of fishes."

"But you would have caught them anyway. And there's only *one* God."

He fixed her with what she was beginning to regard as his "savage look," and said, "It's our way, my Maggie. Our way."

Towaye walked into the water of the sound, and knee-deep in the sluggish current, he stood with spear poised. Maggie couldn't see any fish from where she sat, but periodically, his arm would rise and fall, and as the spear cleared the water, a fish was impaled on the edge of it. With a thrust of his arm, he removed the fish and tossed it into the container by her side.

Watching his muscular body, Maggie had a sense of pride in his prowess, but she still hadn't gotten used to his wearing only the simple, fringed deerskin apron, tied at the waist with thongs. She remained captivated by the suppleness of his body as she gazed in appreciation at the bronze magnificence before her.

Towaye glanced up and caught her watching him, and tossing a final fish into the basket, started toward shore without releasing her gaze. With an effort she looked away, but she felt her face coloring. To hide her confusion she said, "You're an expert fisherman, Towaye. I counted fifteen fish—all big ones. We'll have a feast tonight."

He dropped down on the sand close behind her—too close—and Maggie moved away. He leaned toward her, and caressed her hair with his wet hands. "What were you thinking, Golden Hair?"

The gentleness in his voice when he used the name caused Maggie's pulse to quicken in an inexplicable manner. But she couldn't tell him, and his nearness disturbed her. She had never felt the tug of emotions she was experiencing now. What was it? What made

33

her feel this way? She was afraid of herself, more than of him, but she pulled away from his grasp and stood up.

"I wish you'd wear more clothes. I'm not used to nakedness."

"It's our way. Can't catch fishes wearing many garments."

He shouldered the basket of fish and followed her to the village. All during the preparation of the fish, which he broiled on a rack over a slow-burning fire, Maggie felt Towaye watching her. He knew what she had thought, and she was unprepared for such keen perception on his part. How was she going to cope with him?

If only Richard hadn't gone away, she wished.

CHAPTER 3

NOW THAT THE LARGER GROUP of colonists had traveled north in the pinnace, the few left on Roanoke were without transportation of any kind. Realizing some means of escape was imperative, Topan asked Towaye to help them build a canoe.

"What about the boat we found along the beach?" Maggie asked. But Thomas didn't hear her, and Towaye shook his head warningly. For some reason he must want to keep the others from knowing about that boat, Maggie assumed.

Towaye's methods were slow, but Maggie marveled at the skill of his hands. He directed the colonists to take two cypress trees that had been blown down in a storm, and to cut them into the length of the boat they desired. Towaye was impressed by the rapid severing of the trunk with an ax, and he lifted it time and again to feel the sharp edge.

"My people burn tree in two," he explained. "Slow."

The settlers followed the native custom of burning

out the interior of the tree by igniting resin and gum on the trunk, and then scraping out the coals, but they used an adz for the finishing work.

In case of an evacuation, Thomas knew they couldn't take many possessions, so when two canoes were finished, they ceased their building. The craft were found to be seaworthy in short trips around the island.

Maggie was thankful for the security afforded by those boats when she was awakened two nights later by pounding on their door. She jumped from bed in alarm, and opened the door to peer out into the main part of the dwelling.

Thomas glided noiselessly to the door. "Who is it?" he asked wearily.

"Towaye. A message."

Topan opened the door, and Towaye entered hurriedly, followed by another native Maggie hadn't seen before.

"Runner from my town with message from Peter Colman. Large band of enemies approaching the island from the north. Colman says leave at once."

"How much time do we have?" Topan asked in a calm voice, of which Maggie was proud. Towaye turned to his companion for an answer.

"He not know. Ran as fast as he could, but may be sometime today."

"Towaye," Thomas answered, "go and awaken everyone and fetch them here immediately." As the door closed behind Towaye and the other native, Maggie moved quickly into the room.

"You'd better dress, Maggie. I don't know what we will do, but this sounds serious. Thank God, we have the boats ready."

Maggie was dressed by the time the men had assembled. She wore her more durable clothing—woolen undergarments, as well as a dress and cloak of similar material. She had pulled on heavy hose before buckling heavy leather boots.

"What do you want to do?" Thomas asked the assembly. "Stay and fight, or leave the island?"

"How many Indians?" one man asked.

Thomas turned to Towaye, who shrugged his shoulders. "Many enemies, much more than are here. Better to leave."

"That sounds reasonable," one colonist agreed, "but where will we go? If the Indians are coming from the north, we can't join the other colonists."

Silence pervaded the room as the men tried to assess their position. The only sound was the sputtering of the fire Maggie had tried to rekindle. She looked at Towaye, for she felt his gaze upon her, and he nodded encouragingly. She remembered Richard's words, "You can trust him," and she was heartened by his presence.

"Our nearest haven would be among the friendly natives on Croatoan Island," Thomas said, breaking the silence. "We could stay there until the danger is past, then we could return here, or go to the Chowan area."

No fault was found with that suggestion, and they concerned themselves with the immediacy of the move, each person being dispatched to a task. One man carved a message on a tree for any Englishman to read if a search was made for them. All small guns and powder were loaded into one canoe, and items too bulky to move were buried. Towaye and Maggie packed the foodstuffs they would take with them, and as they were gathering a few coverlets as a last-minute precaution, a shout alerted Towaye. After one quick look, he quietly eased the door shut and put his back to it.

"Too late!" he said, and Maggie's heart seemed almost ready to burst. In that moment, she reasoned that death wasn't far away. For only an instant Towaye stood immobile before he ran to the window, jerked the skin away from the opening, pulled a stool to the wall, and stepping on it, vaulted through the opening. His head reappeared immediately, and he motioned imperiously for Maggie to follow him. As soon as she stepped on the stool, Towaye reached in and pulled her roughly through the hole.

The cabin stood between them and the fight going on at the edge of the settlement, but falcon shots indicated that the Englishmen were defending themselves. Maggie started to speak, but Towaye clapped his hand over her mouth, and lifting her in his arms, ran effortlessly across a cleared field until they reached the shelter of the woods. In the shadow of the deep forest, he gently shoved Maggie to the ground.

"Don't move. Back soon," he said. He glided away through the trees until Maggie lost sight of him. She stayed where she was, too afraid to disobey him, and the rapid thumping of her heart almost suffocated her. It seemed a long time before Towaye returned, carrying Maggie's hood in his hands, which in her haste she'd left behind.

"Cover hair. Show too much." Pulling Maggie upward, Towaye indicated that she should accompany him.

"But shouldn't we stay and help them?" she whispered.

"Too many. I look. Most English dead already."

Towaye took her hand, and she stumbled at his side, sickened by his words. *Uncle Thomas dead! What would she do now?* Time, direction, distance had no meaning for Maggie until daylight dispersed the forest's gloom, and she sensed Towaye's urging for speed. Reaching a small stream that flowed toward the sound, he walked beside it until they came to a boat secured to a cypress tree. Maggie recognized it as the small craft they'd found a few weeks before. Had he secreted this boat thinking they'd need it?

Towaye urged her into the boat, and quickly pushed it away from the bank. Soon they reached the open water of the sound, and glancing warily in every direction, Towaye stood in the center of the boat and poled it toward the mainland. Maggie, sensing his apprehension, glanced fearfully behind her to watch the wooded area near the water. Her fears subsided somewhat as the island grew smaller and smaller in the distance.

Reaching the mainland, Towaye jumped to the beach, secured the boat with nimble movements, took Maggie's hand, and pulled her beside him. Picking her up in his arms, he sprinted up the sandy beach and into the forest.

Not until that moment did Maggie realize how she'd trusted him. "Where are you taking me? To Croatoan?"

"To my village. But not now. We hide today, and travel at night. I know a place."

"Let me walk. I'm too heavy for you to carry far."

"Not going far."

Daylight had fully overtaken them, and the sun was streaking through the tall pine trees when he stopped at last in a sweet-smelling glade. It was still the land where morning dawned, but Maggie was too alarmed to enjoy it. Two pines had uprooted, and their heavy branches formed a canopy on the ground. Towaye lifted a few of the heavy limbs and assisted Maggie in climbing over the foliage until she found an open place between the two large branches. The area was small, but she could sit upright in it, and there was room to stretch her legs. Towaye moved to her side and dropped the heavy branches around them.

The sunlight vanished, but Maggie could still see Towaye as he slid down beside her. The fragrance of pine infiltrated her nostrils, and Maggie knew this place of seclusion might not be too uncomfortable. She just hoped the raiders didn't realize that two of the island's residents had escaped.

Maggie attempted to push from her mind what had happened to the other colonists, and what the future might hold for her. Surely Towaye would take her to the other English settlement as soon as the hostile natives returned to their villages. She didn't look forward to being confined with Towaye in such cramped quarters all day. Leaning back to feign sleep, her eyes flew open again, when Towaye moved closer and took her hand.

"You're mine now, Golden Hair. I saved your life, so you belong to me. It is our way."

As the full import of his words penetrated Maggie's mind, she jerked her hand out of his grasp and stared at him in dismay for a moment before she dropped her head to her folded knees. *What does the man mean? Am I to be his slave? Or worse?*

He had never tried to hide his interest in her—from the first she had known that he was drawn to her. She also knew that she was dealing with a man whose culture was foreign to hers. She couldn't expect him to conduct himself like an Englishman would under similar circumstances, for already she had learned how many of his actions were completely at odds with her beliefs. Maggie was at his mercy, cut off from her own people. *I'll have to use all the cunning I possess to keep him from his purpose, whatever it is.*

Maggie winced as if he'd hit her when she felt Towaye's hand upon her head. "Try to sleep, Golden Hair," he said tenderly. "Must travel as soon as it is dark."

Maggie didn't answer; nor did she indicate that she had heard him. She was afraid to go to sleep with him nearby, and she didn't move. She sensed his removing his hand from her hair, and from the movements she thought he was lying down, but she remained immobile. His nearness disturbed her, and as the silence lengthened, Maggie lifted her head slightly. Towaye was lying on his side with his back to her, and she relaxed a bit. Whatever he intended for her, it apparently wasn't going to happen here.

Leaning back into a half-sitting position, Maggie tried to ease the weariness of her body. A gnawing in her stomach reminded her she hadn't eaten since the night before, and she wondered when she'd have the opportunity again. She knew she could trust Towaye to provide for her material wants, and to protect her from the raiders, but would he protect her from himself? Her thoughts refused to settle until she remembered the promise, "Go into all the world . . . and I'll be with you."

Suddenly Maggie no longer felt alone. God still ruled the world, and she had the assurance of His presence wherever she was. Nothing would happen to her that *He* couldn't handle, and at last she slept.

She awakened with a great start. Towaye was gone! She was afraid of him, but she realized that she was even more afraid without him. What would she do if he abandoned her? But she knew instantly that wouldn't happen. Where was he then? Probably out scouting to see if the way was safe. But the thought persisted, *What will I do if he doesn't return?*

She leaped to her feet, striking her head on a limb when the tree branches rustled, but she sat down in relief when, with a quick movement, Towaye knelt beside her. He pulled the branches back in place, and laid a deerskin pack between them.

"Where have you been?" she demanded.

"To island."

"To the island," she repeated. "Why would you do such a dangerous thing as that?"

41

"Not dangerous for me. The people who attack the English not my enemies. They are gone—traveling north, so we can go soon."

"Uncle Thomas?" she whispered timorously.

"Sorry, my Maggie. Dead. I bury him like the English do. I remember the place, and I'll show you someday."

The tears Maggie had been fighting all day came then, and she didn't protest when Towaye put his arm around her, and drew her head down on his shoulder.

"Don't cry, my Maggie. I take care of you." He patted her head until the crying ceased, then he pulled away from her.

"Must eat, my Maggie. It's a long journey to Winnetoon." He reached into the pack and handed her some dried venison and parched corn. "Eat now, and we get water soon."

She knew this was no time to talk him out of taking her to his village, so she did as he said. And indeed the food did taste good, for it had surely been twenty-four hours since she'd eaten.

"If the raiders are gone, why must we travel at night? I won't be able to see."

"I see. You follow me," he assured her. "After tonight, we go in the daytime, but better be safe now."

Unwisely she touched his arm, and the reproach in his eyes turned to adoration. "I do appreciate the fact that you saved my life and cared for me. It's just that I don't understand what you have in mind. Don't do something that will spoil the gratitude I feel toward you."

He didn't answer, but drew back the pine branches and stepped out into the dusk. He motioned her to join him, and shouldering the deerksin pack, Towaye plunged into the darkness. Maggie's joints, which had become cramped in the hours spent under the tree,

42

soon became limber and walking was easier. As they moved further inland, hardwood trees began to replace the pines, and their thick foliage shut out any light. She followed Towaye simply by listening to his footsteps on the soft forest floor.

Life during the journey consisted of plodding dense forest trails, wading into swamps, crawling through underbrush. Maggie's heavy shoes became sodden with swamp water; her clothes, torn by briers; her body, bruised and sore in every spot. When her skirts dragged through the mud, impeding her progress, and when she stumbled on the long dress, Maggie eyed Towaye covetously. He walked without effort, while her clothes were a burden to her.

Maggie moved in a world of aches and pains, of cold and wet. Towaye talked very little, but she could tell that he was constantly aware of what moved before them, and behind them, in the forest.

"Rest!" became the most precious word in the English language to Maggie. When Towaye said it, she dropped to the ground without a glance at her surroundings. Once she glanced down at her frayed garments, realizing they would never be usable again, and that she had no other clothes. What would she do for garments?

Walk. Crawl. Wade. Step over the log.

Maggie saw the tree root, but she simply didn't have enough strength left to clear it. The fall stunned her, and she didn't try to rise. Hearing her fall, Towaye came to her aid.

"Stand up, only a little more ways to go."

But Maggie had reached the end of her endurance, and she began to cry. "I don't want to get up. Just let me die here. Go on without me."

"No. You go, too. Get up."

"Why should I?" she summoned the courage to

43

say. "If you were taking me to my people, I might find the strength, but I don't want to go to Winnetoon. Take me to the English settlement."

"No, my Maggie," he said, and the savage look crossed his face. "You are mine now. I tell you that."

"What do you want? Make a slave of me?"

"You be my woman, not a slave."

Chills engulfed Maggie. "But you know I'm betrothed to Richard. I've promised to wait." She held up her right hand and showed her ring. "Don't you see? This ring is a symbol of our pledge."

"Richard is gone."

"But he'll return, and I have no intention of facing him with the fact that you've made me your woman," Maggie said fiercely, some of her spirit returning. "That just isn't *our* way, Towaye. I'll never submit to you willingly. Will you force me?"

"No force, my Maggie. Only Englishmen force the women. You'll come to me someday." He touched his chest. "I feel it here. Richard will not come back."

His answer at least lifted one weight from Maggie's mind. If he had no intention of forcing her to be his wife, then she had enough confidence in her own strength that she would resist him to the end.

"Richard will return, and when he does I'll be waiting for him, so why not let me go to the other English?"

Again he shook his head stubbornly. "You are mine. The gods have willed it."

Maggie was still sitting on the ground, and dampness was stealing over her body. "And that's another reason I can't live at Winnetoon. There is only *one* God, and it depresses me to see you throwing those weeds into the air to your many gods. Only *one* God, don't you see?"

Towaye took her by the hand and tugged upward. Maggie didn't budge.

"One big god, but many little ones. It is our way." He seemed to think that phrase explained everything, and Maggie was too tired to persuade him further. He kept tugging on her hand, and Maggie finally rose to her feet. She thought she couldn't walk another step, but with his gentle prodding, they continued their journey.

CHAPTER 4

Dusk gave Maggie her first glimpse of Winnetoon. She saw at a glance that the village was small, about twenty buildings, and situated on a rather large river—but she was too tired to move, let alone appreciate her surroundings.

Towaye led her through the village, deserted except for a few scrawny dogs that barked at their approach, until they came to the largest dwelling. Outside the house a large pot sat over a smoldering fire, and the odor from the pot whetted Maggie's appetite. Towaye had provided food each day, but never had her hunger been sated. Her guide pushed aside a skin opening, and led Maggie inside. A pine torch stuck in the dirt floor provided some light, so that Maggie saw several people sitting on the floor around a clay bowl of food. One young girl jumped to her feet and cried, "Towaye!" No one else spoke.

Speaking so rapidly that Maggie couldn't discern his words, Towaye apparently explained her presence. He pointed to a large woman sitting with legs crossed in front of her. "My mother, Tananda," he said in English. Then he turned to the girl who stood near them: "My sister, Haldonna; she will care for you."

As Maggie's eyes adjusted to the dim light, she suddenly recoiled in horror—every woman in the room was bare-breasted. They wore only the apron-like garment that Towaye used for his attire. Looking down at her muddy and tattered clothes, she was repulsed by the thought, *Will he expect me to dress like that?*

Haldonna took Maggie's hand. Maggie was instantly drawn to the soft-eyed, brown girl, who seemed to be about fifteen years old. Her touch was tender to Maggie's cold, chapped hand, and leading Maggie to the bowl, Haldonna made room for her to sit down.

"You eat?" she said kindly.

Although Maggie's sensibilities recoiled, she sank to her knees and put her fingers into the stew. If she had to stay here, she'd demand a spoon and knife, even an individual bowl.

When Maggie began nodding, and almost fell forward into the food, Towaye muttered something, and Haldonna said, "This way, please."

Maggie looked at Towaye, and he smiled encouragingly.

"Go with Haldonna. You need sleep. Good night, my Maggie."

Maggie followed Haldonna into another room where the torch light didn't penetrate, and she could see nothing, but she sank down on some soft skins Haldonna indicated—odorous, but at the moment Maggie didn't care. She muttered as sleep came quickly, "I'll be with you to the end of the world."

Maggie was awakening, but she didn't want to. She kept fading into a dream world, but her dreams were

47

unpleasant, so at last she opened her eyes. Quickly closing them again, she tried to shut out reality. She was in a tiny room, lying on a shelf fitted into a bark-covered wall. Three other similar shelves lined the walls, but there were no other furnishings.

A door was cut on one side of the room, and she supposed it opened into the general living area of the house where she'd entered last night. When she had stumbled into the room where sleep had put an end to her dilemma, it had been fully dark, but through a small window above her head rays of sunlight were beaming now.

Not knowing what awaited her, but wanting to find out, Maggie threw back the bearskin which covered her and started to sit up. With a moan she fell backward, believing that every part of her body was bruised, and she wondered if she'd ever be able to walk again. Even her feet felt sore and burning. Towaye had been considerate of her, she knew, but several days of unaccustomed walking was more than she could stand.

With a herculean effort, Maggie forced her body up, and she put her feet to the floor. She was still completely clothed, and she lifted her mangled skirts to look at her muddy shoes. The heavy shoes were cut in several places, and she knew they were beyond repair. What would she do for clothes? Her wardrobe, as limited as it had been, seemed commodious now that it was several days distant on Roanoke Island— unless the raiders had destroyed everything.

Her movements must have been heard in the next room, for Towaye immediately entered, followed by Haldonna and two other women. They hadn't bothered to knock, and Maggie concluded she had lost her privacy along with her wardrobe. Was she destined to live out her life in this miniature village, in this hut with many other people?

But the thought intruded, *Isn't this what you wanted to do? Where's your missionary zeal now?* With a wry smile she recalled, *How often the things you pray for come in an unexpected way.*

Towaye mistook her smile for one of welcome, and returned it. The women merely stared. "Good day, my Maggie. Are you rested?"

"No, I'm not rested," she replied grumpily. "My body feels like it's been beaten, and I hurt all over. Besides, I'm dirty. These clothes are ruined, and I don't suppose you have anything else I can wear. I don't mean those things," she motioned to the garments the other women were wearing. "I refuse to go about dressed in that manner; I would die of mortification."

Towaye didn't answer, but left the room, giving an order to one of the women, who followed him, but soon returned with an earthen bowl of steaming water. Haldonna came to Maggie, and said, "We help."

The three women started pulling at her clothes until Maggie pushed them away. "Leave me alone. I can remove my own clothes." She had never stood naked before anyone that she could remember, and she didn't intend to start now. And dirty as her clothes were, they were better than nothing; if she removed them, she doubted ever laying eyes on them again.

The women scattered when Maggie reacted so furiously to their ministrations, and they chattered in their own tongue when Towaye reentered the room. He dropped the leather pack he'd carried on their journey on the bed beside Maggie. Untying the leather thongs, he revealed the contents. Her blue linen dress lay before her. *So this is why he returned to the island!* She lifted wondering eyes to his, before she pushed back the dress and saw some of her undergarments also in the pack. To have this tie with the past was enough, Maggie felt, to ensure her sanity.

"Thank you, Towaye." Her lips trembled, but she kept the tears from coming. "I'll change into this, and surely I can repair my other clothes in some way."

Haldonna left the other women to stand beside Maggie. "I fix," she promised. *So*, Maggie realized *natives understand English better than I knew*. Peter Colman's influence, she supposed. Was he still in the village? Even one Englishman to talk to would relieve her loneliness, but thoughts of Peter Colman fled when she returned her attention to Towaye, and the article he was dangling before her.

"My ring," she cried, recognizing the portion of her betrothal ring that had been entrusted to Thomas Topan. "Where did you get it?" she asked as she snatched it from his hand.

"In the cabin when I was back at the Island. You want?"

"Oh, yes," and she slipped the small gold oval on her finger, snapping it to the section that she held. "You see, Richard has the other piece, and I'll get that the day we're wed."

She lifted Towaye's hand and pressed it to her lips, realizing too late that the gesture was a mistake, for he reached for her and drew her into his arms, clasping her tightly to him. "I told you I'd care for you, my Maggie."

She didn't resist his embrace. After all, she owed her life to him. Being honest, however, Maggie questioned inwardly, *Do you let him hold you because of gratitude, or because you're becoming fond of this man?*

Towaye released her, and left the room, motioning for the women to follow him. Maggie hurriedly removed her soiled outer clothing and began to bathe in the warm water they'd brought. In the midst of her toilet, however, she sensed that she wasn't alone, and she glanced up. Two children were peering in the window, and from the other room of the dwelling, she could see heads pressed against the partition, staring at her through the cracks in the wall.

Angered at first, she suddenly saw the humor of the situation. No doubt the villagers had never seen an Englishwoman before, and she would doubtless be a curiosity to them. She might as well get used to it. She heaped her dirty clothes in a pile, and put on the clean ones that Towaye had apparently gathered in haste. He had gotten only one dress, although he had chosen some stockings and undergarments. But there wasn't a comb, nor a brush, and she felt of her tangled hair in consternation.

As if she'd been waiting for that moment, Haldonna came into the room with a crude wooden comb. Maggie didn't object when the girl started working with her hair, for she noted that Haldonna's own hair was clean and neat. Maggie's curly hair was always hard to manage, but several days of inattention had made it a mass of twisted snarls, and though Haldonna worked patiently, Maggie winced more than once before her hair was hanging neatly over her shoulders.

"Pretty," Haldonna said.

Maggie expressed her thanks, and the girl flashed her a shy smile. She reached a hand to touch the blue linen of Maggie's dress, and patted her fair skin. Hastily she picked up the soiled garments. "We fix," she promised again as she left the room, and Maggie guessed that every article of her clothing would be fingered and examined as they set about repairing and washing it.

Arrayed in clean clothing, Maggie entered the other room determined to face the ordeal before her with optimism. She was stuck here until Richard's return, or until she could persuade Towaye to take her to the other colonists. She might as well make the best of the situation. Perhaps God wanted her to learn as much as

51

she could about the natives—a help to Richard when he established their mission.

On blistered feet she limped to one corner of the room where Towaye sat carving on a piece of wood. Maggie stopped beside him, and he handed her the wooden object—a small spoon similar to the ones they'd used on Roanoke Island.

"Your own," he said simply. He obviously intended to make her life as pleasant as possible, but nothing could atone for the fact that she was being held against her will.

He also handed her a pair of moccasins made with some kind of fur on the inside.

"They feel so soft to my tired feet," Maggie said as she slipped the footwear over her blisters.

Towaye went outside, and soon returned with a small bowl of steaming food. Maggie noticed that there was no fireplace of any kind in the room, so all of the cooking must be done outside. *Unhandy in the wintertime,* she thought.

The food Towaye had brought tasted like porridge, and Maggie tried to assess the ingredients, deciding that some kind of grain had been crushed, then cooked slowly. A cinnamon taste permeated the food, and she asked Towaye what had been used for flavoring.

"Root ground and used for flavor. Good?"

"Yes, I like it."

When she declined another helping, Towaye took the bowl and spoon, rinsed them with water, and wiped them clean with a skin. Placing them on a high shelf, he said, "Yours." Taking her hand, he added, "Come, my Maggie, see Winnetoon."

Walking outside the dwelling, Maggie saw Peter Colman coming toward them accompanied by a native woman. On her back she carried a child with European features. So Peter Colman had taken a wife among the Indians! By now, Maggie was beyond surprise.

"I heard you'd arrived last night," he said to Towaye. "What happened; didn't the Englishmen get my warning?"

"Yes, the message came, but too late. Enemies attacked before they could leave island. All killed except Maggie. I bring her here."

Colman looked appraisingly at Maggie. "You're safe?" he asked, and Maggie surmised he meant more than her physical condition.

"Yes, Towaye has been kind, but the journey here was quite tiresome. Have you heard anything about the other colonists?"

"I guided them to an area northwest of the Chowan River, and they found a site they liked. When I left them, they were building houses and getting ready to settle in for the winter. They're all right, I'm sure."

The woman with Colman was staring at Maggie, and in spite of herself, Maggie stared back. Black hair hung to the woman's shoulders, and a necklace of conch shells reached almost to her waist. Tattooed designs decorated her breasts and arms. She was naked to the waist, and her full bosom gave evidence of the still-nursing child.

Soft leather shoes protected her feet, and a leather skirt covered her stomach and buttocks. She appeared oblivious to the cold wind that was chilling Maggie through her linen dress. Colman wore deerskin breeches, as well as a long-sleeved coat made of the same soft material. His feet were encased in moccasins similar to the ones Maggie wore.

He must have interpreted Maggie's thoughts for he said, "They don't seem to mind the cold weather, but I can't take it. When it's colder they do put on fur robes." And in a reassuring manner, he told Maggie, "You could be in a lot worse hands. These people have welcomed me, and their customs don't differ much from ours." He motioned to his companion.

"She's a good woman, and I'm probably just as content as if I'd taken some English shrew." Maggie wondered fleetingly if he was warning her what she could expect.

The tour of Winnetoon didn't take long despite Maggie's limping gait. A long row of houses faced a cleared field where dried cornstalks rustled in the breeze, and yellow pumpkins still lay among the stalks. The houses were flimsy structures—mostly a framework of poles covered with bark and woven reed mats. One building, larger than the others, stood by itself at the edge of the village, and tall wooden posts with carved heads on them were placed in a circle nearby.

"Our god house," Towaye explained, and Maggie shuddered.

Maggie's attention was drawn to a young woman who leaned against a building in a provocative position. Her ample, high standing breasts were thrust forward, and in addition to the tattooed marks decorating the exposed bosom, she had painted her face and other areas of her body. A pearl necklace dangled down her front, and conch bracelets circled both arms. She would be a temptation to any man, and Maggie was dismayed by her presence. She called to them, but Maggie understood only enough of her words to become curious, and she made up her mind to master the Algonquian tongue as soon as possible. Towaye merely waved his hand and moved on.

"Marona," he explained, "she wants to be my woman." That last statement came as no surprise, and Maggie was suddenly consumed with jealousy of the girl. A tremor of fear passed over her. She certainly didn't want to be Towaye's "woman," but what would her fate be if he took a wife? As young and virile as he was, Towaye wouldn't live a celibate life for long.

Leaving the village behind, Towaye took her hand and smiled affectionately at her as they walked into the forest.

"Feeling better now, my Maggie?"

"Yes, walking has eased some of the sore muscles of my body. That was a long journey for me, but I'll get over it." She knew if she complained too much about the rigors of that journey, he might use it as an argument to keep from taking her to the English settlement.

The towering evergreens and hardwood trees surrounded them, and Maggie was relieved to be out of sight of the village residents for a while.

Towaye sat down on a flat rock and pulled her beside him. She didn't protest when he put his arms around her. She enjoyed feeling his strength, knowing that he would protect her from harm—but would he protect her from himself? And was she strong enough to preserve her virtue? The uncertainty of the future worried Maggie, but for the moment, she simply surrendered to the feeling of security generated in the circle of that strong, brown arm.

Maggie didn't protest either when Towaye turned toward her and lowered his face. For the first time she felt a man's lips touch hers passionately. She expected a feeling of revulsion for she thought, *This man is a savage, a pagan! You're betrothed to Richard; you should hate the touch of any other man.*

But she didn't hate it, and she responded to his seeking lips. A breathless feeling came over her, and she put her arms around him as he pressed her tenderly back on the rock. *Would the kiss never end?* But when Towaye briefly lifted his lips, she gazed into his eyes and wished the moment would last forever. She suddenly pushed him away and jumped to her feet.

"No, I won't let you!" But how could she keep him

from anything he proposed to do? She couldn't run away, and who would take her part against him here in his own village?

"I've told you that under the rules of my church, I'm promised to Richard. You've gone too far. Before any man touches me like you did, he must be my husband. Can't you respect my Christian beliefs?"

Towaye remained on the rock, but he said, "Richard won't come back, but if he does, nothing wrong with what we were doing. Among our people, it's all right to have many lovers before taking one woman for wife. It is our way."

Maggie digested that comment in silence, remembering the words of the preacher who had presided at her betrothal ceremony. "Chastity is one of the new ideas Christianity brought into the world," he had said. That was one thing she must teach to the inhabitants of Virginia. Could she do it by example?

"You want me, I can tell," Towaye continued. "And I must take a woman soon. My mother is sister of our chief, and I may be head man of our village someday. I must have sons. I want you."

Maggie started to say, "I don't want you," but in all honesty, she wasn't sure that was the truth. "Well, you can't have me," she said instead. "Will you promise that you'll never do again what you tried today?"

"Never is a long time. I won't promise. You'll come to me someday, Golden Hair," he said assuredly, and Maggie experienced that weak feeling she always felt at the tenderness in his voice when he called her "Golden Hair."

"No, I won't," she retorted, but she wasn't as confident as she hoped she sounded.

CHAPTER 5

"WHO ARE ALL THE PEOPLE living in your house?" Maggie asked as they neared the village, thinking she may as well learn who her roommates were going to be.

"My mother's sisters, and their children. My brother's wife there, too—she who will soon have a baby. Men are all away now, the hunting season. Winter will soon be here, and we must store up provisions for the cold days."

"You mean there will be more people living in that small house?"

A half-dozen children raced by, rolling pottery balls before them with a webbed racket, while two dogs frolicked at their heels. They didn't differ much from English children in their antics, except the English would have been clothed, while these boys wore nothing but loincloths.

"Some of the women will leave and go to their own lodges when their men return."

"What am I supposed to do?"

57

"You help with the work like other women."

"What kind of work?" Maggie wasn't averse to working, but the domestic training she'd received as a girl wouldn't be much of an asset in an Algonquian village.

"Cook food. In spring you help with the planting. Lots of things to do in summertime."

"In the summer? Are you really serious about keeping me here? I must go to the other English, Towaye."

"You're safer here. Other English settlement will be destroyed like one on Roanoke. As my woman, no one will bother you."

Startled, Maggie stared at him. "Have you heard anything about its being destroyed?"

"No, but will be sometime. Natives don't like so many English to live here."

When they reached the house, he stood aside for Maggie to precede him through the door, and she recognized that he was taking up some of her ways. If she had to stay here, she hoped that she could influence him to change even more of his ways to her style of living.

"What about your father and brother, Towaye? Are they away hunting?"

"No," he said sharply, and his face showed marks of pain. "Father dead, long ago, but brother killed by our enemies when I was in England. When spring arrives, I seek revenge."

"Our people teach that we must love our enemies."

"Strange teaching, my Maggie. Do you love the ones who killed your uncle?"

That was a new thought to Maggie, one she hadn't considered, and she didn't answer. She suspected many of her preconceived beliefs and notions would be sorely tested before this winter was over.

In a short time, Maggie learned that Towaye's

mother, Tananda, ruled the household, and she soon had Maggie working with the rest. She wouldn't have minded the work—it gave her something to occupy her mind—but her feet hurt so badly. The blisters had festered into open sores, and she was becoming alarmed about them.

Within a few days the women had repaired and cleaned Maggie's clothing. "Thank you, Haldonna," Maggie said when the girl proudly presented the garments. The tattered places had been mended with small strings of deerskin, and while the clothing wouldn't have passed a tailor's inspection, the repairs would hold the dress together. Maggie was glad to exchange the lightweight linen dress for the heavier garments.

Haldonna became Maggie's constant companion. Soon after their return to Winnetoon, Towaye left to do his share of the hunting; therefore, the girl's attention was pleasant to Maggie. Haldonna was eager to learn about Maggie's life, and while they worked, they shared confidences about their different lifestyles. Now that colder temperatures had enveloped the village, all the women wore fur robes over their skimpy covering. Maggie was more comfortable now that she no longer had to observe their nudity.

One of the daily tasks was gathering wood, and on Maggie's first journey into the forest with Haldonna, the girl instructed, "Gather small pieces of wood now. Weather is colder, and we have fire inside."

Maggie was pleased to learn that she was having less trouble communicating with the natives than she had suspected. Most of them knew a smattering of English, and with the words of their language she had learned, they had no trouble getting meanings across to each other. Switching from Algonquian to English in one conversation might have appeared comical to an outsider, but it served the purpose well.

"I had wondered if you had to cook outside in the wintertime."

"No, cook inside house. We have little snow, but lots of rain for two-three moons. You have snow in England, Maggie?"

"We have a little snow where I lived, but we have more rain than you have here. And our summers are shorter."

Stooping to pick up a chunk of wood, Haldonna said, "This is kind to take. You hold out arms, and I'll fill with wood." They had to walk quite a distance before they found enough wood for the fire, and Maggie thought how much the Algonquians needed axes, and other tools, to provide their fuel supply.

"How do you get the giant trees to fall?" Maggie asked.

"Burn down," the younger girl replied, and she quickly pushed some pine needles against the trunk of a tree. "Do like this, then set fire by rubbing flint together. Keep fire at edge of tree. Takes many days."

Maggie's mind wandered to the mission that Richard hoped to start, realizing there were many things to teach the natives to make their lives easier. No doubt Richard had noted the need, and would bring some of those supplies back with him.

By the time they returned to the house, a cold rain had started, and Maggie was glad to seek the shelter of the building. A piece of bark had been removed from the roof, and a slow-burning fire was smoldering in the pit underneath the hole. Smoke drifted slowly toward the opening, but the room was still full of smoke, and Maggie longed for the fireplace she'd had on Roanoke Island, as troublesome as it had been.

"Bring vegetables," Tananda ordered when they laid down the wood, and though Maggie had hoped to sit down to ease her feet, she followed Haldonna out into the rain again. She hadn't yet seen Towaye's mother doing anything, and she resented the woman's orders.

"Doesn't your mother do any work?" Maggie asked as they grubbed with a wooden hoe for potatoes in the field opposite the houses.

"Tananda has done her share of work; now it is up to us. Elders do not have to work."

A few other women were seeking supplies in the fields, and they looked curiously at Maggie. The younger people would answer her questions and greetings in halting English, but none of the older persons would speak the foreign tongue.

By bedtime Maggie was pleased to seek the privacy afforded by the attached room, for the sleeping arrangements weren't as bad as she had feared. Haldonna shared the room with her, as well as one other woman, and Cauda, Towaye's sister-in-law, who sat in the corner of the room, all day long, never speaking to anyone.

"She have baby soon," Haldonna explained. "My brother killed in battle few months ago. She mourns for him."

The sound of music the next afternoon announced the hunter's return. An old man, playing a reed flute, preceded the hunters down the main thoroughfare of the village.

"Come, Maggie," Haldonna said. "Big ceremony to thank gods for good hunting."

Almost every man carried a deer over his shoulders. Peter Colman and another man carried a large elk between them, and one boy strutted by with a small buck on his back.

"It is his first hunt," Haldonna explained. "Big day for him to bring home a deer."

Towaye's eyes sought out Maggie as she stood by the building, and she smiled fondly at him. He had changed his loincloth for deerskin garments, and he looked tall and graceful as he stepped along in time to the music.

He lifted his hand in greeting but he continued to walk toward the temple at the edge of the village. When the women and children fell in line behind the men, Maggie followed along to the temple. She hesitated to attend a heathen ceremony, but curiosity moved her along with the others.

The hunters piled their game near the entrance to the temple, and the weroance, one of the tribe's spiritual leaders, danced around the pile of slaughtered animals, playing on his flute, and scattering dried tobacco leaves into the air. Then he entered the temple, and the natives followed.

Their temple was not as barren as the homes, for a stone altar stood at one end of the room, with a fire burning on it.

"Fire burn all the time," Haldonna explained, "to honor our ancestors."

Maggie glanced curiously at the temple as she joined the other women on the left side of the room. Skin tapestries, hanging from the ceiling, were decorated with drawings of animals. Human skulls hung from the wooden posts supporting the building, and seeing them, Maggie felt a sudden wave of nausea. "Our former chiefs," Haldonna pronounced.

The weroance stood before the altar, while the villagers sat on the floor, their legs crossed in front of them. He was dressed in long deerskin breeches, a shawl of feathers hanging from his shoulders to the floor. When he raised his arms to scatter tobacco into the air, the people started chanting, "Praise to the god of thunder, praise to the god of the sun, praise to the god of the moon."

Should I remain here and be a part of this ceremony? Maggie wondered. But she bowed her head and tried to shut out the sounds of their chanting. She forced her mind to dwell on the Scriptures, and the prayer of Solomon when he dedicated the temple came to her mind.

She couldn't remember the exact words, but she knew he had asked that if God's people should be carried away captive, and in the land of their enemies if they should pray, then God should hear their prayer and support their cause. Well, she had been carried captive to the land of her enemies, and in spite of the strange surroundings, Maggie thought God would hear her prayer. Therefore, when the others stood at the close of the ceremony, Maggie stood, too, and as they voiced their praise to the god of the hunt, she recalled Psalm 136, and sang:

Praise ye the Lord, because he is good:
for his mercy endureth forever.
Praise ye the God of gods:
for his mercy endureth forever.
Praise ye the Lord of lords;
for his mercy endureth forever.
Which only doeth great wonders:
for his mercy endureth forever.
Which by his wisdom made the heavens,
for his mercy endureth forever.

The ceremony completed, the worshippers crowded from the room, and as they gathered in groups to chatter, Maggie was reminded of their small Christian congregation in England. She shut her eyes to hold back the tears that threatened to overflow, and she felt a wave of homesickness until Towaye came to her, put his arm around her, and drew her close. No one else in this village ever expressed devotion openly, but he didn't seem to pattern his life from the examples of others; he had a mind of his own.

"All right now after long trip from island?" he said

quietly in an intimate tone that actually made Maggie's pulse quicken.

"Almost," Maggie answered, "except my feet are still sore."

"I'll fix feet," he said. Proudly he led her to the big animal he had killed. "Big deer, I bring in. The hide will make you a cloak for winter days." Shouldering the carcass again, he moved toward their dwelling, where he skinned the animal, and cut the flesh into large chunks.

Marona passed by with some of her friends, and her black eyes surveyed Towaye boldly, as she called seductively, "Ho, Towaye. Meet me at Love Rock?"

He merely waved, and said, "Too busy." Marona gave Maggie a look of pure hate; she had gained an enemy without even trying.

Maggie would have sought the warmth of the smoke-filled house, except she had missed his caring and lovable ways, and she decided to stay with him until Tananda dispatched her upon some errand.

After the meat was prepared, and the women of the household were pounding it and rubbing salt into the flesh, Towaye said, "We fix feet now," ignoring Tananda's sharp demand that Maggie help with the work.

"No! Feet sore. You should have cured. No more work for a few days."

Towaye sat beside her near the fire, and drew off each moccasin, causing Maggie to flinch with pain. Several blisters on each foot were still inflamed and oozed with pus, and Towaye shook his head sympathetically.

"Sorry, my Maggie. Should have told me before."

He took warm water from a pot near the fire, carefully bathed her feet, and from a shelf in the corner, he brought two clay jars. One jar contained a clear liquid he patted on the infected areas, and Maggie winced from the pain.

"Take the poison out, and will make feet better. Now, I put on salve made from wild sage roots and bear grease." The sticky substance had an unpleasant odor, but it did have a soothing effect as he spread the salve thickly over the infected areas.

Wrapping both feet in soft skins, he then helped Maggie to her feet. "Can't walk much now for few days, my Maggie, but feet will be well soon." He drew her close, and for a moment Maggie thought he was going to kiss her again, but he drew away when Tananda entered the room.

Each morning Towaye left soon after they'd eaten, not returning until late in the evening. Haldonna was noncommittal when Maggie inquired about Towaye's activities. With her feet bound as they were, she could do very little, and the days seemed endless. One morning even Haldonna was gone when Maggie awakened.

Limping into the main room to take her bowl from the shelf for breakfast, she asked Tananda in halting Algonquian, "Where is Haldonna?" but the older woman turned her back.

"Why do you hate me?" Maggie demanded, in a sudden flash of anger.

Tananda grabbed her by the arm, and with foul-smelling breath spat the words into Maggie's face, "No good for Towaye. He must have native woman."

The sharp fingers were bruising Maggie's flesh, but she stood without flinching, and answered calmly. "Then we both agree on that. I'm not going to be his woman, and if he would take me, I'd gladly go to where the other English are living."

The older woman shoved Maggie away from her, and turning, muttered, "White liar."

Deprived of Haldonna's cheerful presence, Maggie spent most of the day in the tiny sleeping room, and when she heard Towaye's voice in the outer room at eventide, she hurried to him as quickly as she could. She was glad to see him, but irritated also that he would bring her to this place and practically abandon her.

"Why do you leave me alone all day?"

He lifted a ringlet of hair that was always dangling over her shoulder. "Missed me, my Maggie?"

The acrid smoke from the smoldering fire caused Maggie to cough, and she lifted a hand to wipe away the tears it brought to her eyes. Her clothes smelled like smoke, and her skin was grimy all of the time because the sides of the hut were covered with the black soot that sputtered from the fire. Everything she touched left a dirty mark on her skin. *How can I endure a whole winter of this?*

The next day Maggie's feet were feeling better, and she was tired of being cooped up, so she prepared to take her clothes to the river for washing. Still wearing the heavy skins that Towaye had tied around her feet, she gathered the few garments she had, and headed with slow gait toward the river at the edge of town.

After several days of cold rain, the air was fairly warm again, but the river was frigid, and Maggie shuddered when she put her hands into the water. Choosing a spot downriver from the settlement as she had seen the other women do, Maggie scrubbed vigorously on the soiled garments, but the grime from the cooking fire wasn't easily removed. Lifting a garment from the water for inspection, Maggie shook her head in dismay to see her hands chapped and encrusted with soot, knowing that the icy water would make them even worse.

Maggie was completely hidden from the village, and she spread her garments on the bushes. While waiting for them to dry, she sat awhile in the sun. At times she moved in a world of fantasy, believing her present existence must be a dream; but, sitting on the bank of the river, listening to some noisy crows fighting over grain in the nearby fields, she rationally considered the future.

Richard had been to Winnetoon, so if he returned to the coast, he would probably come looking for her here. But ships didn't brave the Atlantic during the winter months, and by her best calculations, it must be near the first of December now. Therefore, she might as well give up hope that he could possibly arrive for six months.

In the meantime, what would she do? She considered the possibility of asking Peter Colman to take her to the other English settlers, but would he want to jeopardize his friendship with Towaye's people to do that? Was it fair of her to ask him?

And what about Towaye? She was becoming more and more attached to him. Could it be love she felt for this man? Admittedly, she had never loved Richard, but her physical emotions and her thoughts reached out to Towaye. If Richard wasn't to be considered, would she have him? She feared her answer.

Maggie had never been confronted with absolute dislike before, but she knew an important trait of a missionary was to love those to whom one ministered. Marona and Tananda certainly weren't lovable, and she was irritated because she was jealous of Marona and her attentions to Towaye. He didn't seem to pay any heed to her now, but had he at one time? Before Maggie's arrival, had he met Marona at the Love Rock? Even if he had, why should it matter so much to her?

Steps nearby startled Maggie from her reverie. Marona and two other Algonquians were approaching, and struggling to her feet, wishing she were not hampered by the bundlesome skins, Maggie moved to gather her clothes from the bushes. She feared being alone with these women, and wished she hadn't strayed so far from the village.

The three women watched her silently, but when she started back to the village, they blocked her path.

"Don't like us?" Marona asked in broken English.

Maggie said calmly, relieved that her voice didn't betray the rapid beating of her heart, "Please get out of my way."

"Towaye my man." Marona's face twitched in anger.

"That may be. The two of you must decide that. I didn't ask him to bring me here. I want to leave."

The girl's expression reminded Maggie of many shrewish English women she had known. *English and Algonquian—when it comes to love and hate, we aren't so different after all.*

"Go then. We don't want you." Marona slapped her face, and Maggie instinctively lifted her hand to strike back.

"Resist not evil: but whosoever shall smite thee on thy right cheek, turn to him the other also." The verse stopped her. However, when Marona shoved her in the direction of the river, Maggie became alarmed, and dodging around the three women, she tried to escape. Her bound feet hampered her, and in her haste, she stumbled and fell.

The three Algonquians were upon her immediately, and as she was jerked to her feet, Maggie felt the cloth of her garment tear.

They tore her clothes, even those she had just washed, into shreds. Shamed, she stood holding to her the remnants of the dress she wore, watching tearlessly as the last of the blue linen dress floated slowly downstream.

They danced fiendishly around her, and laughing wildly, Marona snatched off her betrothal ring, scratching Maggie's finger in the process. Running to the bank of the river, she threw the ring into the strong current.

Maggie didn't even try to get away now, for she would be ashamed to go back into the village in rags. The cool air was chilling to her body, and Maggie thought the exposure might kill her; she only hoped that her end would come soon.

Pinching Maggie in a tenacious twist, Marona said, "White and ugly. Towaye won't like." While the other women held Maggie, Marona began to prick her arm with a sharp instrument. Maggie's teeth were chattering now from the pain as well as from the frigid air.

"Make you pretty marks on body like us," she said as she wielded the sharp tattooing needle. Maggie glanced down at the design, and endured the burning sensation without comment. "He is brought as a sheep to the slaughter, and as a sheep before her shearer is dumb, so he openeth not his mouth." Remembering the patience of Jesus during His persecution helped her to endure the pain.

Was this sacrifice necessary to reach these people? Must she have her body abused—die for them? As a follower of Christ, could she expect any less than He?

But, God, I hate this girl. Our Lord didn't hate those who taunted Him. Why should I? Maggie closed her eyes and tried to envision the suffering of Jesus when the crown of thorns was forced upon His head, and the pain He had known when the nails were driven through His hands and feet.

Suddenly Marona dropped Maggie's arm, and stepped away from her, for Towaye was running toward them, shouting, "Stop, animals!"

With one blow he knocked Marona to the ground, and as he turned on the two women who held Maggie, they loosed their hold and raced wildly toward the village. Marona scampered to her feet and followed them.

Gathering Maggie into his arms in a protective embrace, he whispered, "Oh, my Maggie, you should have called—would have heard you."

Still Maggie didn't cry, although her body was trembling from the cold and the emotional tension prompted by the incident, but she was afraid no more. Towaye was here.

Towaye shielded her with his body, and patted her tenderly on the shoulder. "Should have been more watchful with Haldonna in Purge House for monthly cleansing. Sorry, Golden Hair." He pressed his lips to her cheek, and the soft movement of his mouth as it caressed her skin brought warmth to Maggie's flesh.

Towaye slipped the fur robe from his shoulders, tenderly wrapping it around Maggie, and he folded it around her before he released her from his arms.

"What did they do to you?" he asked, and Maggie noted, even in that cheerless moment, that his English was improving.

"They tore the clothes I was washing into shreds and threw them into the water."

"All of them?" he questioned, with a glance around the area.

"Just a few pieces of underclothing left back at the house. Do you have anything for me to wear? What will I do?"

"My Maggie can do anything she wants." As her eyes lighted with this unexpected admission, he added quickly, "All but one."

"What's that?"

"Can't leave me, my Maggie. Must stay here at Winnetoon."

"My life may be in danger if I stay here. Marona tried to push me into the river today."

His face hardened. "She not do anymore," he said. "Let's go back to village. I find clothes for you, until Haldonna fix you long skirts of deerskin in a few days."

70

Maggie wondered how many prying eyes followed them down the streets, for she must have looked comical with her torn skirt flapping from beneath the fur robe.

Without a word to Tananda and the other women in the hut, Towaye led her into the bedroom. "Back soon," he promised, and upon his return, he carried a pair of deerskin breeches, and a beautiful tunic-like shirt, fringed with long tassels.

"Legs too long, but roll up," he said. "Try on."

He left the room again, and Maggie was thankful for his consideration; he must know that she wouldn't want him to observe her changing. She did have one chemise left in the room, and she wore it under the deerskin garments. Both the shirt and breeches were too big, but they covered her, and at that moment, nothing else mattered.

"Dressed, my Maggie?" Towaye called, and when she answered affirmatively, he entered the room, carrying a pan of water. He washed away the blood where Marona had pricked her arm, and applied a soothing liquid to it. Smiling encouragingly, he said, "Now let's look at the feet."

He knelt in front of her and carefully removed the wrappings. The sore places had completely healed, and Towaye wiped away the salve that clung to her skin. Maggie had a strange impulse to clasp his head to her, for she was sure that Algonquian men weren't in the habit of ministering to their women as he was doing to her.

When her feet were once again clean and encased in the moccasins he had given her upon her arrival at Winnetoon, he lifted her to stand beside him, and put his arms around her. Looking down at her with a glint of tenderness in his eyes, he said, "Everything all right now, my Maggie?"

"Yes, thank you."

"You are lovely, Golden Hair. Even in rags." Maggie felt her face flushing, but she didn't take offense. He stooped to kiss her full on the lips. His words and action took away her breath, and she eased back down on the bench when he turned abruptly and left the room without giving her time to answer.

CHAPTER 6

THE NEXT MORNING when Towaye prepared to leave the hut, Maggie asked, "Take me with you today. I get lonely here. What do you do every day? None of the other men seem to do anything."

Towaye traced the outline of her chin, moved his hand gently across her lips, and twitched the rebellious lock of hair that was always dangling forward over her right shoulder. Lifting her face to his, he said, "Like to be with me, Golden Hair?" but Maggie lowered her eyelids and wouldn't answer.

"Take some day soon, but not now. Peter Colman going with me today."

Since the incident at the river, Maggie had noted a difference in her treatment in the village. She wondered if Towaye had passed the word that she wasn't to be mistreated. The children and youth even seemed friendly, speaking to her when she greeted them. If Richard and she were to convert the Algonquians, she was certain it would have to be through the children.

Occasionally Maggie faced the possibility that Richard would not return for her, and she would remain in Winnetoon for the rest of her life. Would she be forced then to take Towaye?

"What kind of marriage ceremony do you have?" she asked Haldonna one day when they were alone in the house.

"No ceremony, Maggie. Usually man, or his parents, make deal with the woman. If she agrees, she moves to the man's home. That is all. Sometimes, man goes to woman's home, but not often at Winnetoon."

"I notice that some of the young girls are already married. Many girls younger than you."

"Girls marry thirteen, fourteen years. So far, I don't find anyone I want. We marry within our own clan. Different among English?"

"Yes, of course. It differs from area to area, but after the parents arrange for the marriage, we have a betrothal period when the man and woman become better acquainted—parties, and things like that. Then an exchange of promises, usually a religious service, takes place, binding the two people legally together for life."

"Not our way. Man and woman don't like each other after few years, they separate and find other mates."

This statement startled Maggie—another moral principle to teach them: "for this cause shall a man leave mother and father and cleave unto his wife, and they twaine shall be one flesh."

"Sometimes we have a ring as a sign of our promises to each other," Maggie continued, "like the one I used to wear."

"You're promised to another?" Haldonna was amazed. "Thought you were to be Towaye's woman."

Maggie shook her head emphatically, and the blond

74

curls tumbled around her shoulders. "No, I can't be. I'm promised to another."

"Tananda will be pleased—be trouble with Marona's family if pledge not kept."

"You mean Towaye is pledged to marry Marona?" Maggie questioned, the idea displeasing her. No wonder the girl was antagonistic toward her.

"Yes, two, three seasons ago. Tananda was worried about the house, for Towaye had not yet taken the gift of food to Marona's father."

"What house?" Maggie asked, and Haldonna jumped from her cross-legged position beside the fire; her eyes had a frightened look.

"Don't ask, Maggie. Forgot. A secret."

"Then what do you mean about the food gift?"

"Man supposed to give gift to woman's family before he takes the woman."

Apparently Haldonna reported the conversation to Tananda, for Maggie sensed less resentment from the older woman after that.

Several days of rainy weather had kept Maggie confined in the hut more than she liked, and late one evening when the rain had diminished to a light mist, she went for a walk. The moon lacked a few days being full, but it still shed some light on her path as she meandered toward the forest. The darkness of the woods intimidated her, so she paused, and when she heard footsteps padding along the wet ground, she stepped into the shadow of a tree.

She recognized Towaye, and she started to step out and greet him until she noticed he was carrying the carcass of a deer, and behind him, another man trudged along with a black bear's body weighting his back. Maggie followed them slowly into the village. She stepped back into the shadow of a building when Towaye stopped in front of Marona's house.

"Ho!" he called, and Marona's father opened the skin curtain. Maggie was too far away to hear their words, but after they talked awhile, Towaye left the two carcasses beside the front door. The two men gripped hands in a ceremonial fashion, and Towaye and his companion departed.

Towaye had taken gifts to Marona's family! Was that a sign that he was going to take the woman for a wife? After going to bed that night, a startling thought occurred to Maggie. "How many wives does an Algonquian have?" she whispered quietly to Haldonna.

"Usually one at a time, but can be more if marry within same clan. Why?"

"I just wondered." What would her fate be if Towaye took Marona for his woman? Haldonna's remark about the house suggested that he was building one, and if he moved into another house with Marona, would he expect her to go with them? Maggie couldn't endure the thought.

The next day, as soon as Towaye left the house, Maggie sought out Peter Colman. Although Haldonna had pointed out the small dwelling to Maggie, Maggie had never visited him before.

When she called outside the door, Colman answered, "Enter." Smoke filled the room where the Englishman lounged on a reed mat before the fire, playing with his son, while his woman sat in the background grinding grain with a stone mortar and pestle. Except for his heavy hair and beard, Colman could easily have passed for an Algonquian. Now that the other men of the village were wearing long breeches and shirts in deference to the cold weather, Colman's clothes were just like theirs. He was a short, squat man, and Maggie judged he was probably middle-aged, for a few gray hairs sprinkled his otherwise brown hair.

"Sit," Colman invited.

Maggie dropped down on another reed mat, her feet crossed in front of her. *I've been here long enough, I'm even beginning to act like an Algonquian*, she mused. Like Colman, except for her hair and light coloring, she didn't look a great deal different from the natives. *What would my mother think if she could see me now?*

"How are you getting along, Miss Maggie?" Colman asked in the respectful tone he always used when talking to her.

"All right, I guess, but I can't stay here any longer. Do you know how I can get to the English village?"

"Ain't Towaye treating you right?"

"Oh, it isn't that. He's been wonderful to me, but under the circumstances, I can't stay here."

"Well, I don't know any way you can get to the English settlement either. It's about a week of rough walking, and if you had a guide, you might make it all right, but the weather sometimes gets bad about now. We could have some snow, and it's no time to be wandering in the woods; better stay put until summer."

"Is there any kind of trail to the settlement?"

Colman gave her a keen look. "You ain't intending to try it by yourself, are you? What's happened to put you in such a notion all of a sudden?" he asked.

"Is there a trail to the settlement?" she persisted, ignoring his question.

"Yes, one is used regularly as the tribes go back and forth to trade, or to attend festivals. It starts down by the river, goes north most of the way. But don't try it by yourself, Miss Maggie," Colman cautioned. "When spring comes, if you still want to leave, maybe Towaye will take you to the English."

Maggie pondered leaving for a few days, realizing that she might be foolish to try it. One afternoon when she was alone in the house with Tananda, the woman said quietly, "Want to leave Winnetoon, go to English town?"

Maggie looked up in surprise. Tananda rarely spoke to her, and when she did it was in a strident tone.

"Yes. Yes, I do."

"Be ready in morning. I find guide to take you. Tell no one; Towaye won't like."

After a moment's hesitation, Maggie said, "I'll be ready."

Maggie was thoughtful the rest of the day, and she noticed Towaye watching her all during the evening meal. Did he suspect? *I'll have to be careful,* she thought. *He's wise enough to realize something's going on.*

"Nice evening, my Maggie. Let's walk a bit," he said when they finished eating. Tananda gave her a warning glance as she left the room with Towaye. The light from the almost-full moon was kind to Winnetoon, for the flimsy buildings became fairy-tale dwellings in its radiance. An occasional lacy cloud drifted across the moon, creating spectral shadows on the streets. Would she miss the village after she was gone?

Towaye put his arm around Maggie as they walked slowly. And knowing tomorrow night she would be gone, and he would be disappointed and hurt when he found she'd run away, she slipped her arm around his slender waist.

At this unexpected gesture, Towaye smiled down at her. "Moonlight makes little sparkles of stardust all over your head. *Love!* A word I learn from the English, but I know what it means." He tapped his chest. "Sometimes my heart feels like it will explode and come out. It's love I feel for you, my Maggie."

Fiercely he gathered Maggie into his arms, and because she knew that after tomorrow, she might never see him again, she snuggled close to him. His kisses intensified the trauma of leaving, and her spirit cried out, *It's love I feel for you, too, my Towaye*, but her lips remained silent. If once she allowed the words to be voiced, she knew she could never leave him.

Towaye leaned back until he could look into her eyes. "Someday, Golden Hair?" but Maggie couldn't meet his gaze, and she leaned her head against his chest, lest with his keen perception, he should read the truth in her eyes.

Maggie and Tananda were alone in the house the next morning, Haldonna sent on an errand, when the older woman said, "Quick!" Her sense of urgency lent excitement to her usually emotionless visage.

Maggie went into the bedroom to put on the heavy shoes she'd worn when she came to Winnetoon. She still wore Towaye's breeches because Haldonna hadn't yet finished her deerskin skirt, and because a cool wind was blowing from the west, Maggie took one of the bearskins from her bed. She might need some more covering before she arrived at the English settlement.

Tananda handed her a pack when she entered the main room. "Food!"

Maggie took one last look around the room, remembering the times she had sat beside Towaye, and she wished there was one thing she could take as a remembrance of him. Glancing on the shelf where her personal eating utensils lay, she reached for the spoon. His hands had shaped that, and it wouldn't be heavy to carry; she could keep it as a token of his kindness to her. Maggie slipped the spoon into the pack as Tananda shoved her out the door.

A squat man swathed in bearskin garments stood

outside the dwelling, and Tananda said as way of introduction, "Panamuck, good guide. Go!"

If Maggie had been choosing someone to guide her through the forest, she was sure she wouldn't have chosen this man. He was shifty-eyed, lacking the openness of most of the residents of Winnetoon. She thought she'd seen everyone who lived here, but this man was a stranger to her.

Panamuck started rapidly down the road between the houses, and Maggie trotted to keep up with him. The rapid pace kept her from looking for Towaye, but when they neared the river trail, and the village was almost lost to view, Maggie turned for one last look.

She wondered why the village seemed obscure until she realized that her eyes were filled with tears. Had she really been so unhappy here? How would Towaye feel when he found out she was gone? Momentarily she considered returning, but she didn't think she could spend any more time in Tananda's house when the woman so obviously wanted her to leave. And what if Towaye left her behind when he moved into another house with Marona? No, there was nothing to do but go on. Thus when Panamuck said gruffly in Algonquian, "Hurry," Maggie turned and stumbled after him.

The trail they followed was not heavily traveled, Maggie decided, but it was marked well enough that she believed she could have found the way by herself. When she had followed Towaye from the island, there had been no trail because he had avoided the best-known paths in the interest of their safety. Her days of work at Winnetoon had toughened her, for at the end of the first day she wasn't nearly as tired as she had been when they'd traveled from Roanoke Island.

They camped that night in a forest of huge oak trees, and in the waning light, Maggie gazed through the dried leaves that still clung tenaciously to the limbs, towering upward so that she could hardly see the tops of the trees. She stretched her arms around one of the large trunks and learned that she couldn't span a fourth of the circumference. She loved the forest, and thought that the winter landscape she had seen today was as beautiful as the trees in summer.

Maggie slept very little for, even wrapped with the bearskin, the cold penetrated her body, and morning found her stiff-jointed and chilled. After a hastily eaten meal of parched corn, and the hard bread Tananda had provided, Panamuck motioned her to follow him into the forest on a trail that seemed to follow a westerly direction. When she questioned him, he grunted as if he hadn't understood her. Colman had said the trail to the English village went northward, she was sure.

By late afternoon Maggie was dismayed to feel flakes of snow on her face, and she looked up at the sky, turned a murky gray. They had climbed steadily most of the day, and the temperatures were colder at the higher elevation. Peter Colman had said a week's travel to the English town, so that meant they still had a long way to go. Could she endure several days of this kind of weather? Maggie started to wonder if she should have stayed at Winnetoon.

A light dusting of snow covered the ground by dusk, but Panamuck found an overhanging ledge under which it was partially dry, and he directed her to stop there. The dry earth showed tracks of many small animals, so although Maggie reasoned they were depriving some wildlife of their homes for the night, she was thankful for dry shelter. When she rolled into the bearskin, it was still light enough to see that the snow had increased. What would that do to the trail? But surely Panamuck would know the way.

She awakened to a world of silence and beauty. Dawn was just breaking, and the whole area was blanketed with about six inches of snow, but it was still dry under the ledge. Snug in the bearskin, Maggie peered out into the wonder of the morning. A red bird flitted through the branches of a small evergreen, dislodging tufts of snow that fell to the ground to make artistic indentations in the otherwise undisturbed carpet.

Savoring the beauty and quiet of the spot, wishing Towaye could share it with her, Maggie suddenly realized it was *too* quiet, and she sat up in alarm. She was alone under the ledge. Where was Panamuck? Probably out scouting the route, she decided, and started to lean back in relief until she noted that no footprints in the snow indicated his departure. He had been gone a long time.

She had been abandoned. The thought alarmed her so she broke out into a sweat, and unrolled from the bearskin. All along had it been Tananda's plan to have Panamuck desert her. Tananda thought that her son's attachment to Maggie would prevent him from taking Marona. Too late, Maggie realized how foolish she had been to trust the woman.

Sitting down on the bearskin to assess her situation, Maggie chewed on some dried venison. At first she was unable to accept the fact that she had been deceived—surely Panamuck would return. But after waiting several hours, watching the sun rising higher and higher, glistening on the pure snow, Maggie knew she'd been left to her own resources.

If the trail went northward as Colman had said, as long as the sun was shining, she believed she could keep her sense of direction and find the way. It might melt some of the snow from the trail, she hoped briefly, abandoning the hope when she considered the frigid temperature.

The last thing Maggie did before she left the shelter was to kneel in prayer. "God, I'm claiming Your promise of watching over me. Let the outcome of this day be Your will.'' She closed her prayer by repeating one of her favorite Scripture verses, ''Go therefore, and teach all nations, baptizing them in the name of the Father, and the Son, and the Holy Ghost. Teaching them to observe all things, whatsoever I have commanded you; and lo, I am with you alway, until the end of the world. Amen.'' With more optimism than the occasion warranted, Maggie plunged into the snow.

At first the air and the beautiful surroundings were exhilarating, but her plodding steps became slower and slower. When she felt her strength ebbing, she stopped to nibble on some of the food, noting each time that the supply wasn't sufficient to last a week, as Tananda must have known. Water was no problem, for she simply ate snow when she became thirsty. Would she starve to death or perish from exposure?

Maggie had hoped for some warmth from the afternoon sun, but it only served to blind her with its glare, and as evening approached, the air became so cold that icicles formed on the bearskin in front of her mouth. She tried to keep her hands wrapped in the soft fur, but grasping the pack of food while holding the skin around her impeded her progress, and soon she was gasping for breath with every step.

You're going to perish out here, the thought intruded over and over, but despite the lengthening shadows, and the penetrating cold, Maggie continued to trudge along. *I can't stop. Better to keep going.* She lost all sense of direction, and for all she knew, she might be walking in circles.

Her fatigue caused her to remember how tired she had been when she had traveled with Towaye, and how patient he had been with her. All day she had kept her thoughts away from him, but now that she was barely conscious, his face haunted her.

Maggie reached a hand to wipe icy tears away from her face, and she lost hold of the bearskin, which fell away from her shoulders. Head down, groping for the covering, she suddenly saw a pair of moccasins in her path. Had Panamuck returned for her? But lifting her head slowly, she saw Towaye standing before her. Was she dreaming?

But he was real enough, she knew, when he lifted her in his arms, and without a word, carried her through the forest until he came to a cave. Placing Maggie on the ground, Towaye moved to the front of the shelter, raked a few leaves into a pile and ignited them with a flint, and, adding a few wood chips to the flame, he soon had a fire going. Bringing some branches from the forest, he added those to the flames before he turned to Maggie. He loosened the deerskin bag from her numb fingers and carefully examined her hands. Tired as she was, Maggie glanced expectantly at his face. Was he angry with her?

"No frostbite. Good," he said, speaking for the first time. "Let's take a look at feet now."

Snow and mud had encrusted her boots, and he pulled them off with difficulty. Maggie's feet had been numb for hours, and she was afraid they had frozen, but although they were red and stiff, Towaye seemed satisfied with his inspection. "All right, I think," he said, as he wrapped her feet in the bearskin, and set the shoes near the fire to thaw.

Sitting down beside her and warming her hands with his kisses, he said, "Why so foolish, my Maggie?"

"If you're going to take Marona for your wife, and Tananda doesn't like me either, I just decided to leave. I can't live in a house with either of them."

Towaye's face expressed more surprise than Maggie had ever known him to exhibit. "What made you think I take Marona?"

"Haldonna told me that you were promised to her by your parents, and then I saw you taking some game to her family. When I heard you were building a house, it all seemed to add up."

Towaye shook his head. "Foolish Golden Hair!" he said fondly. "Would you care so much if I took Marona for my woman?"

Maggie's feet and fingers were tingling now that feeling was returning to them, and she wiggled them nervously. She turned her face to the side of the cave, not answering, but taking her face softly in his hands, he made her look at him.

"Took the game to Marona's parents as a sorry gift—sorry I couldn't take their daughter." Maggie was beginning to tremble as the shock of her near-death crept into her mind. Towaye drew her into his arms, wrapped his own bearskin around her, and moved closer to the fire. He held her away from him so that he might look into her face.

"My Maggie, I have told you. Only you for me. You or nobody forever. No need to worry." He lifted her rebellious lock of hair and kissed it.

Maggie leaned her head on his shoulder and surrendered to the soft security of his arms. Darkness had fallen, and they were in a world of their own. Very little of the frigid cold was seeping past the fire that he had built at the mouth of the small cave.

"Must gather some more wood before we sleep. Back in a minute." He left the cave, and Maggie pondered his words. He knew that she would not be his "woman," but he apparently was willing to wait for her to change her mind. Would she ever find such dedication on the part of any Englishman? According to Haldonna, his apparent belief of loving forever was not necessarily an Algonquian trait, so why was this man different from any other she'd known?

Towaye made two trips into the cave with wood

before he was satisfied there was fuel to last them until morning.

"Anything left to eat? Didn't take time to bring food."

"Yes, some corn and venison. Eat all you want; I'm not hungry. I've been nibbling all day." He raised his eyebrows when he found the wooden spoon among the grain, and she felt her face flush. He took only a handful of corn and reclosed the pack.

"How did you learn I was gone?"

"Peter Colman heard it—came and told me. I started out a half-day after you left, but lost trail in snowstorm."

"Are you going to take me to the English town? We must be nearer there than we are to Winnetoon."

His face darkened, and Maggie chilled at his expression. "Not even going in direction of English settlement."

That statement confirmed what Maggie had believed. Tananda had deliberately deceived her. More than ever she felt the need to leave the Algonquian village. "You could stay there, too," she said, knowing she didn't want to be separated from him again.

"No, my Maggie, we go back to Winnetoon. Told you before—English are in danger. You're safer in my village."

"I don't know about that. Marona tried to push me into the river, and Tananda deliberately had me abandoned out here to die."

His black eyes gleamed menacingly in the dark. "No more, my Maggie. Once they know you be my woman, they leave you alone."

"But . . ." Maggie started. He held up his hand.

"My Maggie, the house is for *you*. Been building it to surprise you. We move into it when we return. You won't have to share house with others, just me."

"But I can't be your woman. You know that."

"Yes, I know, but others won't, so you be safe."

For the first time since he had brought her to safety, Maggie's lips trembled, and her eyes brimmed with tears.

"Towaye, I don't deserve you—I really don't. It isn't fair to you, for when Richard returns, I'll have to go with him."

"We'll see; we'll see, my Maggie," he replied wearily. He put another log on the fire. "Time to sleep."

He spread his bearskin robe on the ground, and motioned for her to lie on it. "Must sleep close together to keep warm. Not bother you—you'll be safe." Maggie didn't doubt his word, and she reclined on the skin, while he lay nearby. Covering them both with her bearskin, he placed his arm over her as a shield.

She nuzzled her face against his hand. "Thank you for finding me, Towaye. I owe you my life once more."

"Foolish Golden Hair," he said, and Maggie laughed lightly as she began to grow warm.

The air was still bitterly cold the next morning, and Towaye delayed their departure from the cave. "But we must have food—look around a bit." He was gone almost an hour, but when he returned, his deerskin breeches encrusted with snow, he carried two rabbits. He shivered when he knelt before the fire to brush the snow from his garments.

"If you had to run away, my Maggie, why pick the coldest time of the season?" he chided her. Maggie bit her lip and dropped her head. She wasn't in the mood for a reprimand this morning.

"A lot of trouble for me," Towaye continued, reaching over to tug playfully on her wayward curl, "but worth it all, Golden Hair."

She glanced up and smiled shyly at him as he busily dressed the rabbits, which in a short time, he had prepared and was browning over the fire. Patiently, he turned the rabbits over the coals, and the smell of the cooking meat whetted Maggie's appetite.

"After eating, we travel some today, if you're rested enough."

"Is it very cold outside?" she asked, reluctant to leave the cozy warmth of the cave.

"Yes, but may stay cold for many days this high up. As we get nearer to Winnetoon it will be warmer. We travel a few hours to another place I know where we spend the night. While sun shines, we won't be cold."

When the meat was prepared, Towaye divided one of the rabbits between them, and he wrapped the other in the deerskin bag which was empty now except for the wooden spoon and a few grains of corn. "Keep rest for night," he said.

By high noon they were ready to leave their place of refuge. Maggie looked around the little cave, knowing that it would always be a memorable place for her. Only brown stone walls, dark and unlovely, yet they had provided shelter for her when her life was endangered.

"Could we come back here sometime, Towaye?" she asked.

He regarded her in surprise, she thought, but he said understandingly, "Yes, not far from trail—easy to find." Wrapping her hands in the two rabbit skins that he had cleaned well, and taking the deerskin pack, he ventured out into the bright sunlight.

"Call out if you get tired," he told her.

The snow reached well above Maggie's ankles, but the heavy shoes afforded some protection. The snow was crusted with ice, and as light as she was, Maggie walked on top of the snow sometimes, only to break through and find her feet imprisoned. More than once, Towaye had to pull her from the encrusted holes.

"Should have fetched snowshoes," he said. "Too much hurry, and I forget."

They traveled on ridges as much as possible where the snow seemed lighter, but there were many hills to climb, and Maggie was breathless at the end of each incline. Towaye was considerate of her, and stopped often to rest, and always he helped her up the steepest hills.

Once while they rested, she asked hesitantly, "Who is Panamuck?"

She didn't like the way his face darkened. "Tananda's brother. Wanders the woods, just happened to stop by Winnetoon. Forget him." Maggie said no more, but she was convinced Towaye would not forget the incident.

Throughout the day, Maggie pondered, *Now what?* Three days ago she had thought Winnetoon, and its problems, had been left behind, but now she was heading toward it again. Since all her efforts to leave the village seemed to be thwarted, she considered the alternative: Did God want her to stay at Winnetoon? She remembered how the prophet Jonah had tried to avoid the destination God had intended for him, and that God refused to allow him to have his way.

"God," she whispered, "my faith is still strong, but the way ahead is so clouded. Could You reveal a bit of the future to me? If You only want me to know Your will a day at a time, however, please help me to be patient."

Maggie's spirits lifted after that moment of communion with God, and she thought about what awaited her at Winnetoon. She must question Towaye about the house he had built for her. It must be out of sight of the village, for she hadn't seen any sign of it when she had gone with Haldonna into the forest for wood. And from his comment, he must expect to share the house with her. Though her sense of propriety rebelled, she knew she would be afraid to live alone surrounded by natives, many of whom were her enemies, or at least, most of whom were not her friends.

If Towaye had intended to force himself upon her, he had had ample opportunities, but what did the future hold for either of them this way? Awakening once last night, wrapped securely in the warmth of his arm, her spirit and flesh had reached out toward Towaye, but he was sleeping and had not known. What if he had awakened at that moment and had perceived her willingness? What if the years passed, and Richard didn't return?

She was glad when their stop for the night put an end to her musings. Towaye led her to an overhanging rock where the evidence of earlier fires indicated it was often used by natives.

"Stop here when we hunt sometimes," he said. From their ledge, Maggie looked down a long hollow, partially cleared of trees, to a river that flowed into a small lake in the distance. The snow that blanketed the ground was undisturbed by man, but Maggie could see tracks of animals in the snow near the cave. The rapidly setting sun threw long shadows, making the pine trees appear like giant beanstalks as they etched ghoulish patterns across the snow.

"Big wind take out many trees few years ago," Towaye explained as he built a fire to one side of the shelter, leaving Maggie an unobstructed view of the valley below.

"Feet and hands all right, my Maggie?" he said as he drew her nearer the fire. Maggie had not enjoyed the fetid odor of the uncured rabbit skins around her hands, but they had kept her fingers warm. He helped her remove the frozen shoes and set them near the fire. "Keep feet wrapped in bearskin until shoes dry."

After he had seen to her comfort, he brushed the

snow from his breeches, and unwrapped the long leggings from his slender legs. Maggie hadn't known many men in her twenty years, but she had never known a man who was so considerate of her, of that she was certain.

He intercepted her gaze, and he said softly, "What thinking, my Maggie?"

"About how good you are to me," and she grew breathless as she said it. He leaned over her, and his black eyes were full of meaning—unuttered words that spoke loudly to her. They were on the verge of an intimacy she almost welcomed, which she could initiate with only a word. Silently each searched the soul of the other until Maggie shook her head and looked away.

Wordlessly, Towaye took the rabbit from the deerskin bag, speared it with a pointed stick and held it over the fire. Later, dividing the sizzling meat between them, he said, "May be all we have to eat until we arrive at Winnetoon tomorrow."

"Should I save some of this until morning?" Maggie asked unwillingly, for the long walk had made her ravenous.

"Not if you want to eat it," Towaye said. "Perhaps tomorrow I find something else."

Darkness came quickly, and Maggie sat beside the fire and watched a full moon rise over the horizon beyond the lake, and slowly cast its radiance across the world. Towaye, lounging beside her in a half-sitting position, was silent also, apparently sensitive to the beauty of that moment. As the moon rose higher into the heavens, a star more brilliant than any of the rest gleamed above the lake.

"Towaye, in what direction are we looking?" Maggie asked, reluctant to break the spell of the night.

"Toward ocean."

"Then that's the Star of the East," Maggie said.

"The best I can reckon the time, it must be near the end of December, so that's the star that shone so many years ago and guided the Wise Men to find Jesus." Strange that she should be reminded of that tonight—or perhaps not so strange.

"For the first time in my life, the birth of Jesus seems vivid," she mused. "He was born in a cave, we think, which may have been similar to this one."

"Who is Jesus?" Towaye asked.

Maggie had come to this continent to tell the people about Jesus. Was it only chance that her first opportunity should come under these circumstances?

"Jesus was the Son of God," she began, but Towaye interrupted.

"Which god?"

Trying to choose words that he would understand, she said, "The Great Spirit—the *only* God." For once he didn't argue.

"Although He was the Son of God, He came to earth as a baby. God sent Him to earth to become a man because the people were lost, and He wanted His Son to save them." Maggie paused, but Towaye seemingly didn't find that hard to believe at all. With their great tradition of myths, the Indians were probably more receptive to the idea of Jesus' miraculous birth than civilized people might be. "He was born about sixteen hundred years ago," Maggie went on, "and I believe His birth might have occurred in a place very much like this shelter."

She glanced around as the flickering fire threw dancing shadows in their bare surroundings. *Did Mary have such a small room for the birth of her Child?*

Towaye moved closer to her, pulled her into his embrace, and she leaned against him. "Tell me the story of Jesus, my Maggie."

"He did too many wonderful things to tell in one night, but I'll tell you about His birth. Jesus' mother,

Mary, and her husband, Joseph . . ." she hesitated again, not knowing how to tell of the Virgin birth so that he might find it believable, so she skipped that part of the story.

"They were on a long journey, and when they arrived at the village of Bethlehem, they tried to find a place to spend the night, but all of the houses were full. Finally, they were directed to a cave on the hillside where Mary's Child was born. Outside the village, shepherds . . ." she continued.

"Don't know shepherds," Towaye interrupted.

"Shepherds were men who watched over the sheep. You surely saw some sheep when you were in England—they're animals something like the goats we saw on Roanoke Island." For a moment Maggie's thoughts wandered from the Christmas story as she speculated on what had happened to that small herd of goats, and even the flock of chickens they had left behind on the island.

"Go ahead with story," Towaye said impatiently.

"While the shepherds were watching their flocks that same night, some angels—spirits from heaven— came to tell the shepherds that they should visit the little village to see the Child who had been born there."

Maggie paused, and in her imagination she could see the small band of shepherds coming up the hillside toward them, their sandaled feet slipping on the covering of snow. Perhaps Mary had sat in the circle of Joseph's arm, with the Babe lying on her lap, just as she was now leaning upon Towaye.

"When they saw the Child, the shepherds must have realized that He was no ordinary baby, for they bowed down and worshipped Him." Motioning to the star that was shining more brightly than when she'd started her story, she explained, "Several days later, some Wise Men, maybe like your weroance, came looking for the king. They had traveled a long way by following the star which stopped over the place where Joseph and Mary had taken the Child. The wise men gave Him many gifts."

"A pretty story, my Maggie. Did the Child grow up to be good, or did He turn out bad?"

"Oh, He was good—able to do many wonderful things. He helped sick people, and those in trouble; even brought the dead back to life."

"Not even *one* of our spirits can do that," Towaye solemnly said, obviously much impressed. "I want to hear more about your Jesus, my Maggie. The winter will be long, so you can tell me many stories."

For the first time Maggie thought she had done the work of a missionary. She had already learned through her friendship with Haldonna of the Indians' love for stories, so perhaps this was the way she could teach them the gospel of Jesus.

When Towaye prepared to lie between her and the cave opening, Maggie said, "Let me lie where I can look out across the valley."

"But I must protect you with my body if danger is near. And shouldn't be looking anyway—need to sleep," but as usual he let her do what she requested.

Curled side-by-side in the bearskins, Maggie didn't lie awake long, for her body needed rest, but she awakened the next morning before Towaye did, and again she reacted to the beauty of the valley. The sun had not yet risen, but streaks of light in the east signaled the return of day. Maggie was reminded again of her first impression of this new land, "where morning dawns," as the red ball of the sun peeked over the wooded horizon, and slowly chased away the haze that surrounded them. Maggie could feel no heat from the sun, but the beauty of the moment warmed her.

Towaye made no sound, and Maggie didn't know

how long he had been awake when she felt his gaze upon her. He still looked sleepy, and the black roach of hair stood straight in the crisp morning air. He unrolled from the bearskin in one quick movement, and rekindled the fire.

"Should have called me. Didn't know you were awake."

He sat beside her, and she reached for his hand. "I've been enjoying the beauty of the morning. Your homeland is beautiful, Towaye."

"Yes, but I worry, my Maggie. How long will it stay that way? Will the coming of the English and the Spanish ruin my country?"

Maggie could sense the sorrow of the man, and she had no answer. She knew the attitude of the English toward the natives—scarcely recognizing their humanity. And what would her lot be if she remained with Towaye, either willingly or by force? Any way she looked at it, the future seemed bleak.

CHAPTER 7

THE TEMPERATURES HAD MODERATED, and the snow was beginning to melt, so that day's journey was less strenuous. However, emotional strain had overtaxed Maggie's strength as much as had physical exertion, and she almost looked forward to the return to Winnetoon.

Almost, but not quite. She admitted her contentment at being alone with Towaye, but a reunion with Marona and Tananda would certainly not be as tranquil. How would Towaye's mother react at the news Towaye had circumvented her plan?

But if Maggie were in her own house, perhaps she wouldn't have to see Tananda often. What kind of house had Towaye built? Probably a one-room affair, more like Peter Colman's hut.

Maggie's feet were dragging by the time they reached the river, and she knew that Winnetoon wasn't far away. When they arrived at the path to the village, however, Towaye moved on northward a short distance before walking into the forest.

For a moment Maggie couldn't comprehend her surroundings. From the small clearing where she stood, she could see through the trees the houses of Winnetoon below them. But it was the house that was to be her own that held her spellbound—an exact replica of her Roanoke Island home.

Automatically she followed Towaye as he opened the door, constructed of small poles and daubed with clay. Inside, a fireplace made from river stones covered one wall, a huge oak slab forming a mantel above it. A bedstead covered with skins occupied the opposite side of the cabin, and a table and chairs constructed from heavy logs occupied the center of the room.

She marveled. Towaye had almost precisely duplicated the house provided for her by Uncle Thomas. With the primitive weapons he had at his disposal, his accomplishment was all the more remarkable—but Maggie was speechless.

"For you, Golden Hair. Peter Colman help me."

Remorse caused Maggie to tremble. She had run away from him when he was trying to make her happy; she couldn't be to him what he wanted. It was all too much for her, and she sat down on one of the heavy stools, and laid her head on the rough table while sobs racked her body.

Towaye pulled her upward into his arms to wipe the tears from her face with a tender hand. "Algonquian women don't cry."

Between sniffs, Maggie answered, "And Algonquian men don't pamper their women."

"Pamper?" he questioned.

"Let them have their own way—do what they want," she explained.

"Then I become more mean." He shook her playfully. "Get busy; prepare some food," he said, his voice falsely gruff.

How must he have felt, Maggie wondered, *when he worked to prepare this home for me, only to return to the village and find that I'd run away?*

Towaye started a fire with some wood from a stack piled by the fireplace. Maggie assumed the pottery containers placed nearby contained grain. Several pumpkins and squashes were piled in a corner, and clumps of herbs and dried venison hung from the ceiling.

Maggie watched the fire kindle and the draft pulling the smoke upward through the chimney. No smoke would sting her eyes in this house, unlike in the one on Roanoke Island.

Towaye picked up a pottery container. "Fetch water from the stream. Near darktime now." He paused at the door. "Sorry to bring you back when you wanted to leave, my Maggie, but you have wrapped your hands around my heart. If I lose you, it would be like my heart had been torn from my breast. I love you much, Golden Hair."

Maggie lowered her head so she wouldn't have to watch his departure. *What would happen to his precious heart when Richard returned?* Already she was dreading the inevitable choice she would have to make between him and Towaye. Could she leave him? Could she ever turn her back on the English way of life to become Towaye's woman? An hour later when he came back with the filled waterpot, Maggie hadn't moved, and she still wrestled with the problem. She glanced out the small skin-covered window and noted that darkness had fallen.

Towaye took some ground grain from a container, mixed it with the water he had brought, and stirred it over the fire. Placing a small rack over the flame, he broiled strips of venison. He had provided individual bowls and spoons for them, and he served the gruel into the bowls, and placed one before Maggie. After

98

putting a gourd-dipper filled with water before her, he sat on the other side of the table. He looked awkward sitting there, but Maggie knew that in this house, there wouldn't be any sitting on the floor to eat from a common pot.

They ate in silence, but when she finished her food, Maggie said, "I wish I could do what you want to make you happy—but I can't."

"Maybe someday?"

"I don't know," she admitted. After a pause, she asked, "Would you marry me and live in the English village if I asked you?"

"Maybe, rather than lose you. I want my Maggie to be happy, but we try this way first."

They sat in companionable silence while the fire burned to glowing embers. Maggie's eyes grew heavy, and she knew that sleep wasn't far away, but she wouldn't mention going to bed. After having slept by her side while they were on the trail, would he expect to share her bed? She knew that was impossible, even if he didn't, but he soon made his intentions plain.

"The bed is yours, my Maggie. I will sleep by the door. No one may enter without waking me."

In the shadows near the bed, Maggie undressed and slid underneath the bearskins. Wind was sighing in the pine trees outside the cabin, and a strange sense of peace filled her, but she didn't go to sleep immediately for the future was still too uncertain.

They soon devised a daily routine. When Towaye awakened he kindled the fire, brought water from the river, and helped with the chores—women's work, his tribe would have called it. Maggie prepared the food, but he always saw to it that she had plenty of provisions to cook. Her only other accomplishment was to make some candles from beeswax and bear tallow, so they could have more than the firelight when he worked at night.

His present project seemed important to him. "This will be new garment for you," he said one evening.

"Shouldn't I learn to do that?" Maggie asked him. "I feel useless sitting here while you are always working."

"What do you do in your country in the evening?" he inquired. Apparently when he was in England, he hadn't made much contact with family life, as both he and Haldonna showed the same eagerness to learn about English customs.

"We often had music—my mother could play the harpsichord, and we would sing. Then my father would read to us from the Bible, or some other book. I think I miss the reading more than anything else. It was such a pleasure to me."

Towaye scraped the hide a bit longer in silence. "Been thinking about Roanoke Island. Would it be wrong to go and take things the English left there?"

"But do you think there is anything left?"

"No way to tell unless I return there."

"Several things in our house are mine now that Uncle Thomas is dead. His Bible was lying on the mantle, and some of the tools he had brought along might still be in the house. An ax would make your work much easier, and some of the other implements." Excitement gave a lift to Maggie's spirits. "Would you let me go with you?"

"Hard journey, my Maggie. Better to take some of the men to carry things. Haldonna stay with you."

Her memory of the long journey through the swamps and underbrush told her he was right, but she feared being alone, even for a few days.

"Will think about it." Towaye laid aside the deerskin and came near her. "Promise me you won't run away while I'm gone."

"No, I won't leave." For the most part, during their time alone in the cabin, Towaye had refrained from touching her, but now he drew her into his arms, perhaps also dreading the thought of being separated from her. Several times, however, Maggie had read an unspoken question in his eyes, and his wishes were even more evident now, but she shook her head. "No, Towaye."

He made no reply except to kiss her tenderly, burying his face in her hair. "Smell good, my Maggie." He lifted the long blond curl, and pressed it to his lips. "Someday, Golden Hair?" Maggie didn't reply. How could she, when she didn't know the answer herself?

"How long do you think it will take for Towaye to make the trip to the ocean and back?" Maggie asked Haldonna, who was sitting with her back to the fireplace, sewing a pair of deerskin moccasins.

She looked at Maggie, a slight smile on her face. "You have asked me many times already. Do you miss my brother?"

Maggie felt her face flushing; she hadn't realized she had even spoken the words aloud. She walked aimlessly around the room, listening to the patter of heavy rain on the sides of the cabin. The thatched roof that Towaye had provided was waterproof, and the cabin was dry and warm, but it had been raining for two days, and Maggie felt more than ever like a prisoner.

"This rain will delay them even more." Towaye had left Winnetoon more than a week ago, taking three other young men with him, and Haldonna had been staying with Maggie. Until the rain started they had walked in the forest, spending much of their time outdoors, but the last few days they had spent in the cabin.

Maggie opened the door and peered outside, but a mist of cold rain and the equally cold realization that the clearing remained empty struck her in the face, and she closed the door again. By the fireplace Maggie checked the stew in the pot, although she knew she had stirred the food no more than fifteen minutes ago. She tested the stew, decided it needed more seasoning, and crumbled a few dried sassafras leaves into the pot. Towaye liked his venison stew well seasoned.

"Towaye will be here as soon as he can," Haldonna said. "He not like to stay away from you either." Maggie didn't reply, but she was beginning to think that Haldonna was almost as perceptive as her brother.

It wasn't until she heard the brush of deerskin moccasins on the stone step outside the door that Maggie realized how much she was listening for his footsteps. "There he is," she cried, reaching the door just as it swung open on its leather hinges. Towaye stood on the threshold, and Maggie hesitated only a moment before she rushed into arms that crushed her in a grip so strong that she had difficulty getting her breath. He smelled of the forest, and his wet deerskin garments soaked through her own, chilling her.

Towaye held her at arm's length, and his gleaming eyes took in every detail of her face. "Missed me, Golden Hair?"

"Oh, yes," she admitted, and he pulled her close again, and covered her mouth with a caress so tantalizing that Maggie's blood surged like a mountain cataract as it tumbled down its rocky course. Maggie looked for Haldonna. What must she think of their passionate reunion? An Algonquian would never make a public display of affection. But the girl had wisely disappeared.

Towaye motioned out the door. "See what we bring."

In her delight over his return, Maggie had completely forgotten the reason for his absence.

"Why, Towaye!" Maggie exclaimed. Two of the black and white goats she had discovered on Roanoke Island stood in the clearing, a baby goat by their side. "What a trip you must have had with those animals!"

"Wasn't easy," he admitted. Maggie ran toward them, but the goats shied away from her. The little goat was trembling, though, and Maggie guessed it wasn't very old.

"Carry it most of the way," Towaye said.

The other men were just arriving. Two of them were laden with heavy deerskin packs, but the other man carried a reed crate, and the unmistakable cackling from the crate left no doubt of its contents.

"My chickens!" Maggie cried, trying to peer inside the crate as the men lowered it to the ground. It was too dark to see much, but she made out the hen and three chicks, one of which was screeching in the obvious effort of a young rooster's attempt to crow.

Maggie threw her arms around Towaye again, and said, "Thank you. It will seem more like home now."

"Only for you would I have brought the chickens, my Maggie. Don't like; too noisy. Goats, I like."

"You'll like the chickens, too. In a few years when we've raised a whole flock from these, I'll cook one for you. You'll like chicken better than venison." She stopped abruptly, aware of the significance of her words. Towaye was staring at her, a thoughtful glint in his eyes.

"In a few years?"

Dropping her gaze from him, Maggie was glad it was dark enough to prevent his seeing the sudden rise of color to her face. Had she accepted her role as his permanent companion?

Recovering, she haltingly explained, "Well, I meant that when Richard returns, and we start our mission, we'll have enough fowl so I can cook like we do in England." The words sounded false even to her, and although Maggie wasn't proud of being deceitful, she didn't want Towaye to have any false hopes. She hadn't once thought of Richard when she had made the statement about the chickens, and she was sure Towaye hadn't been deceived at all.

Towaye's companions deposited the deerskin packs inside the cabin and sprinted through the trees toward Winnetoon. With some trouble, Towaye finally secured the two large goats to a tree with some leather thongs, pushed the chicken crate close to the house, and followed Maggie inside.

"Let me serve your food before we see what else you brought," Maggie said, as she hurriedly dished up a bowl of stew. "I thought you'd be back today, and I prepared the stew the way you like it." She also set some cake beside him, a recipe she had concocted from cornmeal, maple syrup, and nuts. Before he started eating, Towaye took her hand, tickling her fingers with soft kisses. "Unhappy when away from you."

She wouldn't meet his gaze, but she knew that she had been unhappy, too. The wind was pelting the cabin with rain again, but she didn't sense the tension of an hour ago. His return had made all the difference between loneliness and contentment.

Later Maggie sat beside Towaye on the floor as he opened the packs. She moved a candle close to them. "Couldn't find much, my Maggie. Most things we buried dug up, but still find all that we could carry."

First, Towaye held up an iron pot, in which he had stored a few pieces of pewter cutlery. He had also brought an ax, and a few carpenter's tools. "Handy in building new houses," he said. He had found a few pieces of Maggie's clothing, even a pair of shoes that she'd given up for lost.

"Towaye, this is wonderful! How can I thank you?" she exclaimed, wishing instantly she hadn't made the comment. Wasn't it obvious?

"One cover not ruined," he said, as he drew out a linen coverlet. Tears stung Maggie's eyes as she fingered the soft material, woven with intricate patterns of hearts intertwined with vines.

"I remember when my mother wove that coverlet," she said. "I was only a child, but I remember the many hours it took her."

Towaye untied the other pack and pushed it toward her, and his dark eyes gleamed proudly. "Your books, Golden Hair."

Maggie's hair tumbled forward over her shoulders as she lifted the few precious volumes he'd brought: a bound copy of *Arabian Nights;* two small books, *Robin Hood* and *The Fool of Gotham;* a velvet-bound children's prayer book; and at last, in the very bottom of the pack, she found the book she desired more than any other.

"A Bible! Oh, Towaye!"

"Important book?"

"Oh, yes. It's God's Word, the Christian's guide for living. I've missed having it to read." She gently leafed through the pages of the Bible.

"Would you read to me?" He reverently touched the strange marks on the pages. Maggie wondered what she should read to a man who had never heard God's word before, and she turned slowly until she came to the fourth chapter of Mark. *Of course! The parable of the sower.* With his agricultural background, he could identify with that story.

"Behold, there went out a sower to sow. And it came to pass as he sowed, that some fell by the wayside, and the fowls of the heaven came and devoured it up. And some fell on stony ground, where it had not much earth, and by and by sprang up, because it had not depth of earth. But as soon as the sun was up, it caught heat, and because it had not root, it withered away. And some fell among the thorns, and thorns grew up and choked it, so that it gave no fruit. Some again fell in good ground, and did yield fruit that sprang up, and grew and it brought forth, some thirty fold, some sixty fold, and some an hundred fold.''

Maggie stopped without reading Jesus' explanation of the parable, but Towaye nodded slowly when she finished. ''True words, my Maggie. I have seen it that way.''

Perhaps sensitive to how difficult it would be for Maggie to deny him anything tonight, Towaye soon pulled his mat near the fire, turned his back on her and went to sleep. Maggie continued reading the Bible, devouring the words that had been denied to her for several months.

When his even breathing indicated that Towaye slept soundly, she quietly moved to replenish the fire, and to ready the cabin for the night. The wavering flame cast soft rays of light on his youthful and serene countenance. Maggie noticed that he no longer shaved his hair into the single roach. Was this another indication of his effort to please her, or was it normal for the men to let their hair grow in the wintertime?

Maggie brought the woven coverlet and tenderly spread it over his relaxed body. He stirred, muttering, ''My Maggie,'' but he didn't awaken. For another hour Maggie sat beside him, her hand gently stroking his outstretched arm. Finally, she lifted his hand, kissed it softly, and moved to her own bed.

Two days after Towaye's return, early in the morning, Haldonna ran excitedly into the house. ''New baby in Tananda's lodge now. Brother's wife had son.''

''It's too bad your brother didn't live to see his son.''

A savage look crossed Haldonna's face, which

reminded Maggie of Towaye when he had one of his contrary streaks. "Bad for enemy. When spring comes, we take revenge."

"Who will?"

"Men of tribe," Haldonna said, anger burning in her eyes. "Must avenge the blood of my brother, and others, too."

Cold chills coursed down Maggie's spine, and she said quickly, "You mean all the men go off to war?" Fear for Towaye made her weak in the knees, and she sat down on the edge of the bed.

"All except the old and sick. Towaye lead the tribe," Haldonna answered with pride.

"Oh, no," Maggie murmured, determining in her heart to turn him from his senseless purpose. Her small band of Believers tended toward pacificism, and she was appalled by the thought of seeking revenge.

Within a few days when Haldonna came for the daily visit, her face was morose, a worried expression in her eyes. "Baby sickly," she said. "He cry a lot—can't keep down milk. Tananda worried."

Maggie tried to take Haldonna's mind off of the baby by showing her the books Towaye had brought from Roanoke Island, and although Haldonna was interested at first, she soon left to see about the trouble at home.

Maggie wandered out into the clearing. She heard the chickens chattering, and she dropped to her knees on the wet earth, and peered at them through the sides of the crate. They seemed none the worse for their trip across the country.

"Hello, my pretties," she said as she crumbled bread for them and dropped it into the crate. "In a few days we'll have a bigger pen for you. I'm expecting a lot of eggs from you in the springtime."

Hearing a step behind her, she looked up into Towaye's face. He had left the cabin early this morning, and she supposed he had been to Winnetoon to check on his family there. Since he was responsible for his mother's household, living apart like this was an inconvenience, Maggie knew, but she was so happy to be in her own house that she couldn't fret about it, especially when Towaye seemed quite content with their living arrangement.

Taking her by the hand, and pointing to the other side of the area, he said, "Little goat die. Trip too much for him, I think."

Maggie looked in concern at the dead animal, but then she turned her attention to the nanny goat, whose udder bulged. "She must be milked."

"Milked?" Towaye asked, shaking his head.

Maggie touched her foot to the swollen udder. "Take out the milk. But she's too wild to stand still while I take care of her. If you'll bring someone from the village to help hold her, I'll be able to milk."

Towaye did as she told him, though he looked skeptical about the whole procedure. With him at the head of the nanny, and Peter Colman holding a vine rope on the rear of the goat, Maggie moved a vessel under the udder and started tugging on the swollen teats.

The goat stirred uneasily, seeming about as skeptical of the situation as Towaye was, and Maggie guessed she had never been milked before. Only Colman appreciated her efforts.

"I'll drink a gourdful of that when you're finished, Miss Maggie. Been a long time since I've tasted any milk."

Maggie's struggle was rewarded with about a pint of milk. The goat was nervous and would hardly give down the milk, and it had been a long time since Maggie had tried to milk an animal, so her fingers balked at the unaccustomed chore.

When the news of Maggie's milking got out, a large

group of Winnetoon's men and children gathered each morning in the clearing to watch the process.

"Miss Maggie," Colman said one day when she'd gotten a large portion of milk, "why don't you take some of this fresh milk down to that baby in Tananda's lodge? The babe is dying, I think, and probably from lack of nourishment. I remember that goat's milk is supposed to be good for newborn babes."

Towaye had resisted all Maggie's urgings to drink the milk, though he had gingerly tested some of the products she had made from it. One morning when she had found an egg in the chicken's pen, she made a cake by using the milk and the egg, adding maple sugar and some dried currants. Haldonna ate a piece of the cake so greedily that Towaye consented to try some, and he admitted, "Very good, my Maggie. Like some more," and Maggie laid another slice of cake on the wooden slab before him. But how would he react to giving some of the fresh milk to the newest member of his clan?

"Maybe," he said when Maggie told him what Colman had proposed. "Don't want baby to die. Need some children in the family—nobody left but Haldonna and me."

"You go with me to the lodge then, for Tananda probably won't let me feed the baby." Maggie took some of the milk in a small pottery urn, and carried a pewter spoon with her.

She hadn't gone to the village since Towaye had brought her back after Tananda's attempt to lose her in the wilderness. Maggie had forgotten how unpleasant life could be in one of their lodges until she entered the smoky room.

No wonder the baby is sick, she thought, as smoke stung her eyes. Cauda sat near the fire holding the mewling infant in her arms.

"Going to give the boy some of the milk," Towaye said in Algonquian, his voice carrying enough authority so none of the women objected. Maggie knelt beside the child, and taking a small amount of milk in the spoon, she gently inserted the liquid between the child's bluish lips. Working slowly, but patiently, in an hour Maggie had forced a good part of the container's contents into the child's mouth. She paused periodically to be sure the child retained the liquid.

Early the next morning, Haldonna burst into the house. "Baby better. Tananda want more milk."

Each morning Maggie took fresh milk to the lodge of Tananda and fed the babe. When she thought that Cauda could feed the child, Maggie stopped going, and sent the milk with Haldonna. Soon the child started to gain weight, and to take on the healthy bloom of a growing child. Maggie could sense a change in Tananda's attitude toward her, although the older woman still evidently resented Maggie's presence in the village.

CHAPTER 8

Soon after the baby's crisis ended, Maggie invited Haldonna to their cabin for her first English lessons.

When Towaye noticed her efforts, he brought her a large slab of slate, obtained in some past trading excursion, along with some small chalklike rocks from the creek. Maggie was delighted to have some way of marking the letters and numbers for Haldonna to learn. The girl proved an apt pupil, and Maggie worked diligently with her. During the lessons, Towaye always stayed in the cabin, and Maggie guessed that he was learning as much as his sister. The long winter had promised to stretch before Maggie, but now she had a purpose for being at Winnetoon.

"Maggie," Haldonna asked one day after she had finished her lessons. "The children of Winnetoon would like to learn. Why not they study with me?"

"Why, of course," Maggie agreed, and soon she had more than a dozen children and youth gathered in her house each afternoon. Occasionally, apparently intrigued by stories they heard from their children, a few women would slip in unobtrusively to listen.

Not unlike Englishwomen, Maggie reflected, observing the pride on the mothers' faces when their children recited a story they had heard. They listened closely as Maggie read the stories of Jesus. One of their favorites was the story of Jesus' feeding of the five thousand. It was a great day for Maggie when some of them learned to read the words for themselves.

Throughout the winter, many residents of Winnetoon came to "Maggie's House"—but never did Tananda and Marona put in an appearance. Peter Colman and his family came often in the evening, and by the light of the fire and the sputtering candles, Maggie read to them from her meager store of literature. Colman could not read, but he wanted his son to learn.

"I'm glad you're here, Miss Maggie," he told her. "When my son is old enough to learn, I want him to read English. Europeans are going to take over this country, and in order to survive, he'll have to think like an Englishman."

"But I don't intend to be here that long," she told him. "If Richard doesn't come for me this summer, I'm going to the English village anyway. I can't live like this forever."

"Ain't Towaye good to you?" Colman asked in surprise, and Maggie knew that he assumed like the rest of the village that she was Towaye's "woman."

"Of course, he's good to me, but I'm betrothed to Richard Shabedge, and if he returns, I'll have to marry him. Towaye has known that all along."

Colman shook his head, even shaggier than usual. "You could be making a mistake, you know, although I admit that there are times when I think about my own kind with longing. I may even leave someday."

"Will you tell me before you leave? If Richard hasn't returned by then, take me with you back to the other English colonists."

But Colman wouldn't promise.

All winter Towaye had worked on the dress for Maggie, and she had observed with interest. The project had seemed to take forever, but now he was almost finished. Maggie watched the dexterous movement of his hands as he fitted pieces of birdskin, with the feathers still attached, and sewed them together with silk grass and finely divided deer sinew.

"What kind of feathers have you used?" she asked one day.

"Most of the dress is made from green feathers found on heads of mallard ducks. Look pretty with your hair."

"Poor birds!" Maggie said. "A lot of them had to be killed for that many feathers."

"Tribe has to eat something, so might as well use feathers, too." Truly the natives rarely wasted anything, using every piece of bone and skin from an animal, as well as the meat for food.

Maggie passed the winter days by taking care of the goats and the chickens, cooking for Towaye, and teaching the children of Winnetoon. Often as she lay in bed, listening to Towaye's deep breaths of sleep emanating from the other side of the room, she worried about the coming of summer.

The season was apt to bring two events to cause her trouble—Richard would return for her, and Towaye would go off to war. What if Richard returned while Towaye was away? If she should leave with Richard, how would Towaye feel when he returned? More and more she thought about her family in England.

One night as they sat by the fire, Towaye worked on her dress, and Maggie read to him from the Gospel of Matthew, ending with the words, "Teaching them to observe all things, whatsoever I have commanded you, and lo, I am with you alway, until the end of the world."

Towaye commented, "You talk of the mission Richard will start here. What is the purpose?" Maggie noted that Towaye's English was more fluent, and she marveled at the change in him in a few months. She actually believed he was *thinking* more like the English.

"He wanted to tell the natives about Jesus, and also teach them the English way—a better way of life."

"How better?" Towaye asked, not looking at her, but plying the sharp needle through the skins before him.

"How to read and write, how to adapt our customs to your way of life; how to use metal tools for your work instead of bone and wooden implements; how to domesticate animals."

"All the things you have done this winter?"

Maggie looked quickly at him. *Why hadn't it occurred to her that she had been doing the work of a missionary? Was this the way God had willed it?* Seemingly so, and Maggie wished she could be reconciled to the idea that she was doing what God expected of her. But periodically the longing to be among her own people came over her, and she dreamed of seeing her parents or Jane Pierce again.

Maggie didn't answer Towaye's question. Instead she said, "When springtime arrives, will you take me to the English settlement?"

Towaye raised his head quickly, apparently surprised that she still wanted to leave. He shook his head negatively. "Too busy then. You not happy here?" His arm motioned around the room.

"It's not that . . ." she paused as he waited impatiently, "You have no right to hold me against my will." *But do you want to leave?* Her conscience asked for honesty, but she ignored the probing thought. "You didn't like it when the English took you away."

"Can't leave. You are mine, my Maggie. I saved your life when others were killed; you belong to me," he asserted firmly, but Maggie's irritation over his obstinacy ebbed when she saw the hurt and disappointment in his eyes.

"Tananda says soon I cannot come for my lessons," Haldonna said as she helped Maggie place the precious books on a shelf after the day's study was finished.

"Why not?" Maggie asked quickly, realizing she would miss these daily sessions. Had Tananda thought of something else to irritate her?

"Soon time to plant crops, and during the summer, we have festivals, work in fields, all sorts of things. Maybe study next winter?"

"Maybe so," Maggie answered absently, pondering where she would be next winter.

Maggie was ready with an idea when Haldonna came the next day. "Do you think we could have a celebration to mark the end of our studies? We could have some special treat to eat and have you and some of the other children read or tell stories you've learned. We could invite the older people."

Towaye was listening. "Good idea, my Maggie, but crowded in cabin."

"If it's a pretty day, we could have it outside."

The students worked busily on their "pieces" over the next few days. Maggie wanted to work in as many Bible stories as possible, while she tried to make the program an entertaining one.

"Going to fix some cake?" Towaye asked.

"Yes, if the hen will just cooperate and lay some eggs. It's been a month since I've gotten an egg." She had hoarded a few of the eggs, however, and in a couple of days, Maggie was able to make enough cakes for every resident of Winnetoon to enjoy a small chunk.

"Help me crack some of these nuts, Towaye," Maggie said the night before the program when she started fretting that they might not have enough to eat. She placed some grains of corn into the iron pot and popped them into flaky white morsels, then taking some currants and the nuts Towaye had provided, she melted maple sugar and poured it over the ingredients and formed the resulting sticky mixture into small balls.

"Sample one of them, Towaye, and tell me if they're good," she said when the goodies were solid enough to eat.

"Good, my Maggie," He reached for another one, but she smacked his hand.

"No, only one for now. And you're not to eat another one tomorrow until our guests have all had one."

"Don't be bossy, Golden Hair." But he didn't take another.

The program was scheduled for the afternoon, and although the morning dawned cool and crisp, Towaye predicted that the afternoon's temperature would be pleasant enough. Taking him with her, Maggie went into the forest to gather evergreens to place around the improvised stage.

In some rocky soil near a swiftly moving stream, they came upon some dark-green vines covered with pink and white flowers. "Oh, look," Maggie cried, "Those are the first flowers I've seen since last summer. I want to take some of them to intermingle with the evergreens." Maggie held them to her face, inhaling their spicy fragrance.

"Arbutus," Towaye said. "Always bloom in late winter. You like?"

"Yes, they're pretty, and they smell good, too."

"Tananda knows story about the arbutus."

"Then maybe she'll tell me the story this afternoon. Will you ask her?"

He seemed a bit doubtful. "Maybe," was all he would promise.

The program was going well, Maggie thought. Haldonna was the announcer, and she spoke first in English, then translated into Algonquian for the benefit of those who couldn't understand the foreign tongue. Maggie was gratified at the older people's obvious appreciation of this sign of knowledge from one of their own tribe. Much to Maggie's surprise, even Tananda and Marona had come. In fact, it seemed the whole village was in attendance.

By way of introduction, one small boy recited in halting English, "For God so loved the world that He hath given His only begotten son that whosoever believeth in Him should not perish but have everlasting life."

Next came a group of small boys who presented "Midge, the Miller's Son," an episode from the tales of Robin Hood. The boys acted out the antics of Robin Hood and his three friends, who intended to play a joke on the miller's son. Although the boys spoke their lines in English, Haldonna interpreted into the native's language.

"Midge, the miller's son," she explained, "was walking along the road with a sack of ground grain when he was stopped by Robin Hood and three of his friends. The four men thought to play a joke on the boy by pretending they were going to rob him, but he grabbed handfuls of the flour, threw it into their faces, and while they were blinded from the grain, he began to beat them over the backs with his heavy staff."

The men smiled broadly, and a few of them even laughed aloud as they contemplated that turn of events. The enjoyment of the Algonquians was not surprising, especially when one considered their forest surroundings.

"Robin Hood had to be rescued by a large troupe of his men," Haldonna continued, "but instead of punishing the boy, Robin invited him to join his tribe because he needed brave men to fight with him."

One of the older boys, who had been unable to learn much English, had been delighted to hear the stories from the Bible, and he told the story of the Good Samaritan in his own tongue. The natives apparently found it easy to transfer the roles of priest and levite to their own religious leaders, for many of the older men nodded sagely when the outcast helped the man in need. Maggie wondered what the weroance thought of the story, for he sat to one side, shoulders hunched over, listening intently.

The program was finished, except for a closing song, and Maggie whispered to Towaye, "Is Tananda going to tell her story?"

"I think so. Let me ask her," and while he conferred with his mother, Maggie grouped all the children around her and sang a hymn that had been a favorite with her congregation in England. She had translated one verse into Algonquian, and she thought the older people listened carefully to the message of that verse.

So, Lord, when that last morning breaks,
Looking to which we sigh and pray,
O may it to thy minstrels prove
The dawning of a better day.

Noting the intensity on the faces before her, Maggie knew she had chosen the song well. Although she was sure that they, like Towaye, believed in many gods, they did look forward to life after death. Like the parable of the sower, she had sown some seeds today. *How much of it has fallen upon fertile soil?* she contemplated.

118

The children sat down, and Tananda rose ponderously to walk to the stage. Sitting cross-legged before them, she began, "Many moons ago, an old man lived in a lodge deep in the forest. The world was wrapped in winter; snow and ice were everywhere, and the old man wore many furs.

"His fire was low, and he sat huddled over the flame, listening to the snowstorm as it whirled and roared by his lodge. As the coals turned to white ashes, the wind blew open the door of the lodge, and a beautiful maiden entered. Her cheeks were like the wild rose, her eyes glowed like the stars in springtime, and her hair was as yellow as the pumpkin blossom."

One small child standing near Maggie reached out to touch her hair; apparently she reminded him of the maiden.

Tananda's voice rose in volume. "Her dress was of green grass, her moccasins were of white lilies, and on her head, she wore a crown of violets. Her breath caused the air to become warm and beautiful.

"The old man was pleased to see the beautiful maiden, and he said, 'I am Manitou, the god of the earth. My breath can make the rivers stop, and the waters become hard as rocks.'

"The maiden smiled. 'When I blow my breath about me,' she said, 'flowers grow in the fields, and the rivers start singing songs of joy.'"

As Tananda changed her voice to resemble the voices of an old man, and then again until it took on the vibrant melodies of a young maiden, Maggie could almost feel the change from winter to springtime.

"'When I run through the forest, all run before me,' the old warrior continued. 'The animals hide in their dens, and the birds leave the lakes and ponds and fly to distant lands.'

"'But when I pass by,' the maiden said, 'the forest becomes bright and joyful. The animals leave their

119

holes; the birds return to the waters; the leaves come back to the trees. And wherever I put my feet, flowers grow profusely.'

"After a while the old man's face grew silent, and he slept, enabling the maiden to see more clearly the face before her—the icy visage of winter. Slowly the old man's body shrank and dwindled, vanishing into the earth, and his clothing turned to fragrant flowers. Then the maiden moved away, stooping often to place flowers on the ground.

" 'Whoever plucks these, my most precious flowers, must do so upon bended knees,' she said, and," Tananda concluded her story, "those flowers can be found only in the places where she left them. That beautiful maiden, Springtime, left the trailing arbutus for the Algonquian."

Maggie knew that she would always remember the fascinating tale of the passing of winter into springtime. When she tried to compliment Tananda on her presentation, the older woman merely nodded her head. She had obviously told the story for the love of it—not to please Maggie.

The tribesmen reluctantly accepted the foreign food Maggie and Haldonna offered them, but the smacking of lips and their chatter soon told Maggie they relished it.

Sinking to her haunches, Maggie leaned back against the wall of the cabin. The party was over.

"Tired, Golden Hair?" Towaye asked as he sat beside her.

"Yes, but content, too. Everyone seemed to have a good time, and I did enjoy Tananda's story. I'm interested in your heritage, Towaye."

Drawing her head to his shoulder, Towaye smoothed the golden curls that had become ruffled during the busy afternoon. "I love my Golden Hair.

You are good for my people. Become one of us," he said in a beseeching tone that almost caused Maggie's will to falter. There was one obvious way for her to become an Algonquian, and Maggie interpreted his wishes.

"No, Towaye; you are dear to me, and I've enjoyed teaching the children, but nothing has changed. I must wait."

CHAPTER 9

ALMOST AS IF TANANDA'S LEGEND had been a forecast, spring came quickly and chased winter from the forest. The willows along the river were the first to put forth green leaves, followed by the red maples and poplars.

By Maggie's calculations, it was early May before the oak trees showed signs of leafing, time for the Algonquians to start their spring planting. But the rains postponed the planting of corn, and for some reason, Towaye was fretting about the delay.

One rainy night he brought three jars into the house, and after their evening meal, he sat near the fireplace, the containers in front of him. In one jar he placed some limestone, in another some black mineral which looked like coal, and some small rocks streaked with red were dropped in the third pot. With stone pestles he ground the minerals until they became powdery enough to sift through his hands.

When she finished putting the food away for the night, Maggie sat near him on a mat drawn close to the fire. She drew a red fox shawl around her shoulders for the night air was still cool.

"What are you doing?"

"Making paint," Towaye answered without looking up. "Supply about gone."

"But why do you need paint?"

"For ceremonies. Lots to do in Winnetoon now that spring has arrived. Paint body."

"Is there any particular significance to the colors?" she asked, thinking that sometimes it was next to impossible to get any information from him.

Towaye poured water into the three containers and mixed them slowly until they were smooth. Shaping the black paint into a cake, he said, "Black represents death and mourning; white means peace; red is the color for war and strength."

The word, *war*, shattered Maggie's serenity. With the arrival of warm days, and nothing having been said about fighting, she assumed that the war of revenge had been abandoned.

"You aren't going to fight because of what happened a year ago, are you? Towaye, be reasonable. You're supposed to love your enemies; that's the Christian way."

He gave her a pert look. "You don't love Marona."

Maggie's face grew warm. "Marona is not my enemy. I've long forgiven her for destroying my clothes. You're just trying to get away from the subject. Will you give up this senseless idea of going to war?"

"It's our way, my Maggie," he said, a term Maggie hadn't heard for a long time. More and more, he was succumbing to her ways. She had thought her influence might even have changed his desire for revenge.

"But what's going to happen to me if you go to war and get killed?"

He had shaped the paint into bricks, and he placed them in the ashes of the fireplace, stacking a few sticks of wood over them to kindle a steady blaze. "You can go to the English settlement then—don't want to be my woman anyway."

Annoyed, Maggie stood up. "And what's to keep me from leaving while you're off fighting? I may do that if you go away. I'll find someone to show me the way."

He caught her arm, and his eyes darkened ominously. "No! You won't run away." He released her, and Maggie turned her back on him and prepared for bed. It was the only time they had quarreled, and it disturbed her.

Towaye was gone when Maggie arose the next morning, and she went about her duties woodenly. The cakes of paint lay cooling on the hearth. The thought crossed her mind to throw them away, but she knew, when his "savage" side erupted, as it had last night, she dared not irritate him.

By the time the soil had dried enough for planting, Towaye had gotten over his belligerence, and he took her to the fields which surrounded Winnetoon. Deciding both of them had been afflicted with "cabin fever," she tried to forget the incident.

"Which field is yours?" Maggie asked as they joined most of the other Winnetoon residents on the opposite side of the river, which they crossed in small canoes. A new area had been cleared by burning off the trees, and they were grubbing out the stumps to get the soil ready for planting.

"No one owner. Whole tribe produces crops and shares them. That way no one goes hungry."

"That way some can be lazy and get away with it, too."

"Not happen often among our people. Good way to work it."

By the time they crossed the river, the men were already breaking up the soil with wooden hoes and spades. Towaye joined them, and while the men prepared the soil, the women sat in a group and chattered while they sorted the seeds.

Haldonna sat near Maggie. "When ground ready," she said, "we make holes about this far apart." She held her arms to indicate approximately three feet. "Then we put four grains of corn in the hole. We plant beans, squash, pumpkins, and sunflower seeds between rows of corn."

Maggie did her share of the work, and once when Towaye went by, he patted her approvingly on the shoulder. He had told her she didn't have to go to the field, but the fact that she had joined them for the work had pleased him.

When the sun was high overhead, the workers stopped for lunch. Each woman had brought some food to share, and Haldonna proudly passed around Maggie's nut bread, baked with her scarce eggs and milk.

After eating, the people lounged on the ground, and one man pulled a reed flute from his garments and started a rollicking tune on it. Several of the men, and then the women, sang legends of the past, about Algonquian men who had performed herculean feats to overcome fierce animals or the forces of nature.

One man jumped to his feet and danced in rhythm to the music in steps that reminded Maggie of an Irish jig. Maggie laughed with the rest, and for the moment, she didn't feel like a stranger, but one in spirit with the people of Winnetoon. She felt Towaye's eyes upon her with the unspoken question in his eyes. Would she ever *have* him as her mate?

No, I can't, she thought. She was promised to another. In her heart she felt Richard would return, and her Christian convictions told her there was more to marriage than Towaye seemed to realize. Towaye must have interpreted her thoughts and her struggle, for he looked away in disappointment when he discerned the answer in her eyes.

"Now, we have the spring festival," Haldonna said excitedly when they finished the last field of corn. "Lots of fun then."

Maggie had learned much from Haldonna about the social life of the village, and she was looking forward to the first celebration.

Since Maggie's goat milk had saved the baby's life, and since the day of the program, Tananda had looked more kindly upon her, so Maggie entered into the annual spring festivities. She went through the ritualistic cleansing of the home when the inside fire was extinguished, and the building scrubbed. But she refused to drink the cathartic drink, used ceremonially as a purge to rid one of evil spirits.

"You should drink it, Maggie," Haldonna advised. "A good way to get rid of your sins, and to also insure a good growing season."

"Jesus died to take away our sins," Maggie answered, but Haldonna looked uncomprehending, causing Maggie to wonder how much of the seed she had planted through her lessons had fallen upon stony ground.

The day before the festival, visitors from neighboring clans started coming to the village. Curious about the newcomers, Maggie sat with Haldonna in front of Tananda's house to watch the arrivals. In appearance they varied hardly at all from the residents of Winnetoon, but Haldonna identified the various clans for Maggie by pointing out the different tattoo markings and the paint on their skins.

"What are all these people going to eat?" Maggie asked Haldonna as they shelled peas for their evening meal.

"Towaye and others are hunting now. Will be big feast tomorrow."

The next morning Maggie dressed in the feather garment Towaye had made for her. The dress hung straight from her shoulders to below her knees, by English standards an odd-looking garment. Still, he had made it especially for her.

"Pretty," Towaye said as he held a sheet of mica for her to view the effect. The mica only produced a blurred image, but she could see well enough to comb her hair into an orderly clump at the base of her neck. Feeling self-conscious in the dress, Maggie nonetheless walked with Towaye to observe the many activities in Winnetoon.

Near the temple area, poles stuck into the ground in a circle formation were decorated with stalks of dried corn. Even at that early hour, men waited in line to enter the circle. Others were already leaping around the poles, waving sheaves of dried stalks, shaking gourd rattles, and singing high-pitched refrains.

Adjacent to the temple grounds, a group of boys played a ball game. "Explain the games to me," Maggie said, noting that few females were to be seen.

"This one, very simple," Towaye replied, motioning. "It's a game for ten players, and each one has a pole." Maggie noted that each participant held a pole about six feet long.

"See," Towaye continued, "large stone disks must be hurled on their edge, and in a straight line, to the far end of the clearing. Each person has to hit the disk with the pole, or at least to place the pole as close as possible to the stone when it stops."

"This looks like fun," Maggie observed as they watched a small group of boys using netted rackets to catch and throw a ball.

"Fun, but dangerous," Towaye agreed. "More than once, someone gets hit with the racket. Sometimes on purpose, when one team loses."

"No women seem to participate in games, I notice."

"Women supposed to be cooking food for the men," he said, and his look was a bit reproachful.

A stroke of conscience smote Maggie. She didn't intend to be contrary, and she would have helped with the cooking if he'd asked her. "Would you rather I acted like an Algonquian woman?"

His eyes deliberately scanned her face, pausing momentarily on her lips, and his gaze was so warm that he might as well have kissed her. "If I had wanted an Algonquian woman, would have been much easier than the trouble it's caused me to keep you. No, my Maggie, you captured my heart the first time I see you on the boat coming from England. Only you for me."

Peter Colman and his small family wandered by, and Maggie was glad to change the subject. "Does this remind you of market day in England?" she asked Colman.

"A right smart, it does, Miss Maggie." And to Towaye, "Tried your hand at anything yet?"

"Thought I might race a bit, or shoot the arrow," he said as he patted the bow slung over his shoulder.

Before they reached the edge of the village, where foot races were being run along the river bank, Towaye stopped to observe a game of chance. Two players were competing in a contest. One man held a clump of split-reed sticks, all less than a foot long. With one sweep of his hand he threw down part of the sticks he held, and the opposing player had to guess the correct number as soon as they hit the ground.

"Ho, Towaye," a visiting tribesman hailed him. "Accept my challenge."

Towaye stopped, and for three successive times, he called out the correct number of sticks thrown to the ground. The visitor drew an arrow from his quiver, and handed it to Towaye, who motioned Maggie to follow him. Maggie squeezed his hand. "I'm proud of you, Towaye," she said, and he smiled at her.

Maggie could hardly believe that this was quiet Winnetoon, for sounds of laughter, music, and talking echoed throughout the river valley. Towaye won two of the foot races, but he lost the next two.

Disgruntled, he said, "Your fault, my Maggie. Feed me too much English food. Not strong like I used to be."

"Nonsense! Anything I've fed you would only make you stronger. You're just older than most of these boys who are running. How old are you anyway?"

"I have seen twenty-five summers, my Maggie. How many for you? I have often wondered."

"Well, why didn't you ask then?" Maggie laughed as she said it. "My summers have been twenty. My birthday is the first day of June, which would be about now. I've lost exact count of the days."

Upon their return to the village, Maggie went to sit on the grass with the other women, while Towaye sat with the men. The day was warm, and the women had shed their outer robes, almost all sitting bare-breasted. Maggie felt the outsider again, and her face burned when Marona taunted her, "Feather dress no good at festival."

Weary of the antagonism of the girl, Maggie said, "Oh, Marona, why don't we try to get along? I don't want to be your enemy."

"Don't like you," Marona said sarcastically, tossing her shoulder-length black hair. "Took my man."

"I've told you before: it was Towaye's idea to bring me here. I would have gone to the English long ago, but he won't let me. And I'm sorry you don't like me. I like you," Maggie said, and prayed it was the truth. Marona snorted and turned away.

Maggie determined anew to make friends with the girl, especially since Towaye seemed to think that the tense relations with Marona were a flaw in her Christian witness.

Although the day was given over to games and feasting, when evening came, the Indians crowded into the small temple to share myths and stories of their ancestors. Maggie listened intently to learn about the religious beliefs of the Algonquians.

A ceremonial fire burned in the center of the room, and the weroance, and two other men, hovered over it. Maggie couldn't follow all of the narrative, but she gleaned that the Indians' supreme spirit was usually called Manitou, one without form and having little contact with men. The Great Manitou was an ever present emotive force that took second place to the nature spirits who ruled the Indians' daily lives.

Maggie wondered how old the weroance was, for he looked like a gnome, small and shrunken as he was, and his raspy voice emitted trembling monotone sentences. He asked a blessing from the mighty forces of the spirits that drove rivers, danced upon the rain clouds, whisked through the trees, and brought changes to the earth in spring and autumn. He begged for favors from the five spirits who blessed the food crops—sisters who often rustled among the corn to touch the stems of squash and pumpkins.

"The first people," he said as he droned on about the creation of the world, "lived above the sky because there was no earth. When the chief's daughter fell ill, the chief was advised to dig up a tree and place his daughter beside the hole. During the digging, the tree fell through the hole dragging the girl with it.

"The girl fell downward into an endless sheet of water, where two swans supported her body because she was too beautiful to be allowed to perish. Great Turtle was the master of all the animals, and he called a council to decide what to do with the woman. It was decided to build an island for her to live upon, and animal after animal dove to the great depths of the water to bring back dirt and pile it upon the back of Great Turtle to form an island. As soon as it was big enough, the two swans placed the woman upon the island supported by the great waters."

The weroance paused, and Maggie's mind wandered as she glanced around the room. The natives were enthralled with the story, although she was sure they'd heard it many times before. Maggie squirmed in her cross-legged position. No one else seemed uncomfortable, but she couldn't become accustomed to sitting like this. She uncrossed her legs and spread them out a bit, nudging Tananda in the process, which earned her a cross look. Even Towaye frowned at her from his position across the room, so she became reconciled to discomfort, and listened to the rest of the story.

"But the world was dark," the weroance continued, "so the animals decided they must put a great light in the sky, and finally Little Turtle agreed to climb the dangerous path to the heavens where a great black cloud was emitting lightning. Little Turtle climbed around the cloud collecting the lightning as she went, and making a big bright ball of it, she threw it into the sky, and called it *sun*. Because she thought there should be more light, she gathered a smaller amount and made another ball, which became the moon. Then the burrowing animals made holes in the corners of the sky so that the sun and moon could go down through one and up through the other as they traveled to make day and night."

As the lengthy story continued, Maggie compared his story to the creation account of Genesis. The similarities were too obvious to ignore. Had the natives made some contact with European religions already? Legends had circulated throughout England about Irish monks who had crossed the seas in the ninth century. Had that been more than a legend, and had those monks taught Towaye's ancestors about God? Or had God simply revealed a measure of truth to this primitive tribe of people? "God," Maggie whispered, "can Richard and I take what they already believe, and teach them about Your Son?"

The morning stillness was broken by pounding on the door, and Maggie sat up in alarm as Towaye rolled off his mat by the fireplace, and in one quick movement reached the door.

Haldonna tumbled into the room. "Enemies attack the village," she cried breathlessly, and her frightened face brought a chill to Maggie's body.

"Stay here—bar door," Towaye ordered, as he grabbed his bow and headed out into the predawn light.

Two days had passed since the spring festival, and the village had returned to its normal tranquility. No one, obviously, had suspected an enemy approach.

Maggie quickly donned her heavy deerskin skirt and vest. "What has happened?" she inquired sharply.

"Tananda says the same tribe attacked last spring and killed my brother. We do not know they were near until they set one house on fire. Tananda very angry with Towaye—been trying to get him to raid their village to pay back for death of my brother."

And I've been counseling him to love his enemies. Just last night she'd read to him from the book of Matthew, "Ye have heard that it hath been said, Thou shalt love thy neighbor, and hate thine enemy. But I say to you, love your enemies: bless them that curse you: do good to them that hate you, and pray for them which hurt you, and persecute you, that ye may be the

132

children of your Father that is in heaven: for He maketh his sun to arise on the evil, and the good."

Shut off as they were from the village by the trees, the two women couldn't see anything, but occasionally they could hear shouts wafting through the window. At last Maggie thought she couldn't bear the suspense any longer. "I'm going to find out what is happening."

Haldonna ran to the door and spread her arms wide across it. "No! Towaye not like. Very dangerous."

Advancing on her, Maggie said, "It's dangerous for us here, too, if the raiders come this way. We don't have anything to protect ourselves if an enemy tries to force his way in here."

Haldonna reached under her skirt, and withdrew a thin-bladed knife, which she threw to Maggie, hilt first. Maggie let the knife drop to the floor, and she stepped away from it, remembering that she'd been taught that fighting was not the way to achieve peace.

"You won't act that way if you're attacked," Haldonna said, with a hint of the obstinacy that Maggie sometimes noted in Towaye.

Suddenly the door burst open with one mighty shove, causing Haldonna to stumble and fall to her knees. Towaye stood in the opening, his visage marred by anger. He moved toward Maggie, and she shrank from the venom in his eyes.

For the first time she feared this man who suddenly seemed like a stranger to her. Maggie retreated until the wall stopped her, and when Towaye came nearer, he grasped her vest in his hands and pulled her toward him until only a few inches separated their faces.

"So I must love my enemies," he grated out between taut lips. "You have stolen my manhood. I have become a shame to my family, a coward to my enemies. To please you, I have avoided making my enemies pay for slaying my brother, and so they have attacked again. No longer afraid of us, they dare to invade Winnetoon and kill our women and children. Enough of your peace talk, enough of your Christian ways. From now on, I will be *all* Algonquian. It is *our* way that will be followed from now on." He thrust her away from him with a force that sent her reeling until she collapsed on the floor.

How ironic, that in the moment when he renounced her and her ways he had never before spoken the English language so fluently.

Maggie remained on the floor, watching in silence as Towaye gathered several of his personal items and left the house without looking her way again. When the door closed behind him, Maggie glanced at Haldonna who had also remained immobile during her brother's bitter tirade.

"Towaye angry," she said unnecessarily.

Maggie rose wearily to her feet, trembling, not knowing if her weakness was caused by fear or the fact that she hadn't eaten for many hours.

"Do you suppose we dare go and find out what has happened?" she asked Haldonna.

The girl jumped quickly to her feet. "I go—you stay here," and she picked up the knife and thrust it into Maggie's hand. "Enemy probably gone, but you keep anyway. Towaye not want to lose you."

But Maggie wasn't sure about that now. She stirred the fire, and the gruel was almost ready by the time Haldonna returned with news that destroyed Maggie's appetite.

Haldonna's face was ashen, and although she had no tears, her voice was lifeless. "Bad! Two houses burned. One boy killed. Marona, too."

"Marona killed?" and Haldonna gravely nodded her head. Maggie's hand clutched her throat. She had waited too long to make friends with the girl. Would Towaye blame her for Marona's death?

No one had died in the village since Maggie's arrival at Winnetoon, and she didn't know how the natives would react to death. Not sure of her welcome, Maggie went with Haldonna at sunset to the home of Marona's parents.

The girl's body was lying on a mat in the center of the hut, dressed in a new deerskin skirt, her bare bosom decorated with the conch-shell jewelry and pearls she had loved to flaunt. Blood had been cleansed from the gash where the arrow had pierced her heart, and a small patch of deerskin had been placed over the wound. Women and children crowded the small room, along with Marona's parents, to keep vigil over the still body. Special mourners were painted with black paint, and their disconsolate wailings throughout the night were almost more than Maggie could bear, but she stayed there and suffered with them.

The next morning Maggie followed the others to a secluded area along the river where the men had dug a deep hole in the earth. Still lying on the reed mat, Marona's body was laid carefully in the hole, which the old women had lined with bark. Bowls of food were placed in the grave, small sticks placed over the body, and a deerskin covering was spread over the sticks before the grave was filled with dirt. The weroance pranced around the grave, shaking his gourd rattles, and muttering incantations that Maggie was too tired to try to understand.

Her tears were genuine as she mourned the wasted life of the girl, who had apparently loved living so much, but as she looked around the gathered mourners, no one else was shedding tears. Their faces were emotionless. Maggie refrained from looking at Towaye. Was he sorry now that he hadn't taken Marona for his wife? Did he wish that the girl was back from the grave? Was he angry with her, or angry at himself? Maggie's heart was burdened. He hadn't spoken to her since the attack, and she needed his understanding to help with her own guilt. Why had she avoided Marona all these months?

Maggie didn't stay for the burial of the child. She had witnessed all the grief she could take in one day. Sitting on the steps of her house, and watching, without really seeing, the chickens scratching in the pine needles, Maggie contemplated the immortality of the soul. Thrust upon her own, without anyone to guide her spiritual nourishment, she realized she needed some guidance, too. How difficult to teach others when she also had a need to learn.

Were the natives' somber and emotionless attitudes in the face of death an indication of their lack of faith in immortality? The preparations for burial, interring the deceased's possessions so that she might have them in the next world, indicated that they did believe in life after death. Still the possibility of reaching them with the truth of the resurrection of Christ seemed remote.

The stillness that had fallen over Winnetoon after the death of its residents was suddenly broken by shouting in the village, and fearing that the raiders had struck again, Maggie ran quickly to peer through the trees. The shouting came from the temple area, where with torches held high, the young men of the village were dancing around the sacred circle of poles, brandishing war hatchets, and carrying spears and arrows. They ranted and raved—their shouts grating on Maggie's nerves—and she ran to Tananda's lodge, where she found Haldonna watching the dance.

"What is it?" Maggie demanded.

"War dance. Warriors preparing to go to battle."

Maggie fled to her cabin. Could she dissuade Towaye from seeking revenge? Did she have any right to?

His sudden appearance at the cabin startled her, for in her agitation, she hadn't been aware that the shouting of the war dance had ceased. She opened her mouth to plead with him to forgo vengeance, but his appearance intimidated her. His head had been shaved, only the black roach down the center remaining. His body reeked with the smell of bear grease, and was streaked with red paint. Although he had continued to wear deerskin breeches even after the coming of spring, she thought in consideration for her displeasure of nudity, he was naked now except for a brief loincloth that hung from his waist in front, and was tied with thongs around his thighs.

She stared at him, horror-stricken, until he broke the silence. "Get things. Go to Tananda's lodge till I return."

There was no use arguing, and she really didn't want to stay at the cabin if he wasn't there. She gathered a few personal belongings, and stood awaiting his further command. Before they left the cabin, he came close and held her eyes with a piercing gaze.

"Don't try to run away. Promise."

Although she didn't have the will power to break her gaze from his tense inspection, she didn't say a word, nor indicate by any gesture that she would obey him. Not until this moment did she realize that she had given up hope of changing him—one way or another, she was going to leave Winnetoon.

He must have read her thoughts, for he pulled her toward him, and bent her backward in an embrace. The intensity of his passion overwhelmed Maggie, and as his lips bruised hers, she suddenly realized with misgiving that despite his savage nature, she loved this man with a violence that equalled his. A tremor swept over her body, as he stirred stormy impulses within her, and she returned his fierce caresses. For a fleeting moment, she thought of offering herself as an incentive to keep him at home.

"You are mine, Golden Hair—don't forget it." The words were familiar, but the old tender tone was gone. At this moment he was all Algonquian. She hadn't fazed him at all.

Haldonna looked oddly at Maggie when they arrived at Tananda's lodge, and Maggie glanced down at her garments, which were smeared with bear grease and red paint. She lifted a hand to her face, and it came away red and oily. What had happened at the cabin must be obvious to everyone.

Towaye lifted her head until he could look into her eyes, and he said softly in the tone he habitually used in addressing her, "It is our way, my Maggie. *Our* way." And then he was gone.

CHAPTER 10

PETER COLMAN WAS SITTING in front of his hut. Maggie had passed his woman on the way to the river for water, so she came to the point quickly while Colman was alone.

"I have to get away from here before the warriors return. Please take me to the English settlement."

He shook his head. "I won't do it, Miss Maggie. It ain't safe for either of us to be out in the woods now. In the spring when these Indians go on the warpath, they'll attack anybody."

"Then give me directions, and I'll go by myself. I'm more afraid to stay here than to be alone in the forest."

Colman shook his head even more emphatically. "No, you wouldn't make it, and I'd feel responsible for your death. Why not try to be content here?" he counseled her. "You should count yourself lucky that you fell into Towaye's hands. Among many tribes, you would have been reduced to a slave or a harlot. Towaye has been so good to you that he's estranged the rest of the tribe at times."

Knowing that she wouldn't get any help from Colman, Maggie turned her back and walked away, blinking back the tears. A pall of waiting seemed to hang over the village; even the children played silently.

For a couple of days Maggie pondered her escape. The main reason she wanted to leave Winnetoon, she knew, was that her defenses against Towaye had weakened often enough until she was actually afraid that she might forget all of her religious and moral standards and submit to him. She had to get away before he returned.

If she could find her way to the English settlement, she would take the first boat she could find back to England. If Richard hadn't already left the country, she would tell him how impossible it was to spread the gospel among the American natives. As far as she could determine, their dream was no more than that— just a dream. Someday Christian Indians might become a reality, but not now.

Knowing that Colman was right, that it would be foolhardy for her to strike out by herself, Maggie finally settled down to await Towaye's return. She went daily with Haldonna to the corn fields, feeling she must keep busy at some task. She brought her books from the cabin, and whenever possible, she gathered the children around her and read to them.

More than a fortnight passed before a child ran down the streets of the village announcing the return of the warriors. Maggie almost feared their return. What if Towaye was not among them? What if he had fallen captive, or had been killed in battle? And in her heart, Maggie knew if an enemy arrow had taken the life of the one who had become essential to her happiness, life would never be the same.

He was not in the first group to enter the village, and Maggie's legs began to tremble—the palms of her hands moistened. The shouts of the warriors were obviously plaudits of victory, indicating that the tribe had exacted the vengeance it had sought. But where was Towaye?

At last he came into sight along the river, bearing a burden on his back. At first Maggie thought he was carrying the body of a dead man, and she supposed it was one of the tribesmen who had been killed. But she soon saw that the burden was a live one, and by the tattooed markings on his body, Maggie recognized that this man was a stranger, a captive taken in battle.

Towaye's eyes searched until they found Maggie standing behind Tananda, and he smiled briefly, relief mirrored in his eyes. Maggie's gaze was drawn to the prisoner, who couldn't have been more than Haldonna's age.

"Great day for Towaye to bring home a prisoner," his sister said proudly.

"But what will he do with a captive? Make a slave of him?"

Haldonna motioned for Maggie to follow her as the villagers crowded around the returning warriors. "Maybe keep to replace one of our warriors, but may kill him, his life to pay for the death of my brother. It is our way."

"*Our* way, *our* way," Maggie cried. "I have become weary of hearing that phrase. Just because you've always done something doesn't make it right. That boy probably had nothing at all to do with the death of your brother."

Towaye deposited the prisoner on the ground in the sacred circle. He winced from the deep wound on his thigh as Towaye drew him to his feet, and tied him to a stake. Then the victorious warriors danced around the boy brandishing their weapons in a victory dance, shouting, "Manitou bring the victory."

Horror-stricken, Maggie watched the scene, fearing

for the boy's life. But one by one the men left the scene and wandered toward the river, whereupon the other villagers began to harass the prisoner. Women spat on him, the children pelted him with stones, and through it all, the boy stood without flinching. In appearance, he wasn't much different from the residents of Winnetoon, and he seemed a little older than she'd thought at first.

Watching the persecution of the boy sickened Maggie, and she fled to her cabin, where she lay on the bed, trying to shut out the sight of the scene she'd witnessed. More than an hour passed before she heard Towaye's steps, and she sat up to stare at him. A ceremonial bath in the river had removed all of the red stain, and his loincloth had been replaced by long deerskin breeches.

"I'm hungry, my Maggie," he said as if he had just been gone for a few hours and expected a meal to be waiting for him.

"Then you'll have to go to Tananda's house. If you remember, you ordered me to stay with her. There hasn't been a fire here since you left."

"I remember other things, too," he remarked, and Maggie knew he was referring to the scene between them when he had kissed her, and she had responded to his caresses. She refused to look at him, and he turned toward the fireplace to kindle a blaze.

"Sorry I became angry, my Maggie. Sorry I was rough with you." His voice was tender as before, but Maggie couldn't forget those tumultuous incidents they'd shared before he had gone away. She was afraid to trust him now, never knowing when he might turn on her again. Perhaps recognizing that she had no intention of cooking for him, he took dried strips of venison from the shelf and warmed them over the low blaze.

"What are you going to do with that boy?" she demanded.

"Nothing now. Tribe will decide in few days. No concern of yours, my Maggie."

Haldonna stuck her head in the open door. "Tananda wants to know if all right to feed prisoner."

When Towaye nodded, Maggie hurried off the bed. "I'll go with you," she said, and darted out the door before Towaye could refuse.

Haldonna took a bowl of stew from the simmering pot in front of Tananda's lodge, and Maggie walked with her to where the prisoner was tied. Towaye was already in the sacred circle when they arrived, and, when he untied the thongs that held the boy erect, he sank to the ground in exhaustion.

The boy ate as though he was ravenous, and Maggie ran back to Tananda's house for a bowl of water. The prisoner raised grateful eyes to her as she handed him the water, and in that moment, she made up her mind to save him if she could.

The wound in his thigh was festering, and ignoring Towaye, she poured some of the water on the infected area.

"Haldonna, bring some of the ointment from Tananda's lodge. I'm going to dress this wound." When Towaye offered no objection, the girl raced swiftly to her mother's house. By the time she returned, Maggie had cleansed the wound.

"What is your name?" Maggie asked in Algonquian, but with a look at Towaye, the boy refused to answer. She felt sure he had understood what she had said. The boy stared at her blond hair and blue eyes. No doubt she was the first European he had seen. Towaye allowed the prisoner to remain seated on the ground, but he tied him securely to the post, and set a guard of two men around him.

Haldonna was strangely quiet as she walked with Maggie away from the prisoner. "Feel sorry," she said.

"Are you finding it difficult to hate your enemies?" Maggie said gently, easing her arm around Haldonna's shoulders. Haldonna didn't answer, but Maggie speculated that she might be able to enlist Haldonna's help in releasing the prisoner some night. The thought entered her mind that if she helped him to escape, the whole tribe might turn on *her*, but regardless, she couldn't stand by and allow them to kill the boy.

Several days passed, and no attempt was made to dispatch the prisoner, and in those days, a change came over Haldonna. She carried the boy's daily provision to him, and whenever she could, Maggie went with her. She watched the exchange of glances, the timid touch of hands as Haldonna gave the boy his food. Occasionally they whispered so softly Maggie couldn't hear.

But her plans for releasing the prisoner were no nearer to accomplishment than they had been at first, for Towaye had changed his sleeping place. Instead of placing his mat near the fireplace, he spread it across the doorway, and Maggie couldn't determine whether he was doing that to prevent *her* escape, or whether he knew what she contemplated about the prisoner.

"His name is Little Raven, and his tribe is far to the north. He not fight in battle yet; never killed anyone," Haldonna reported. She had come to Maggie's home to beg some goodies for the prisoner. "He like the cakes I take two days ago," she said. "Do you have more ready?"

Ten days had passed since the return of the victorious warriors, and Maggie wondered how much longer the boy would be kept alive. He remained tied to the post in the sacred circle, and Haldonna had not tried to hide her interest in him from Maggie.

Wrapping the pastries in a soft skin, Maggie watched the girl's heightened color with sadness.

"Has Towaye said what he will do with the prisoner?" Haldonna asked.

"No, he won't talk to me about it—says it's none of my concern." She caught Haldonna's hand. "Don't become too attached to the boy, my dear. I fear for his life."

"But I don't want him to die, Maggie. He is so young, so kind. I have thought about helping him escape, but someone is on guard all the time." Her beseeching eyes stirred new remorse in Maggie's heart.

Nodding her head, Maggie said, "I know. I have had the same thought, and apparently Towaye senses it, for he's slept across the doorway since the boy has been here. There's no way I can get out the door without awakening him."

Haldonna went away, her slender shoulders sagging as if she carried a weight too heavy for her immature years. *Why did she have to become fond of this prisoner?* Maggie reflected. *Is love always so painful?*

The next morning when Towaye finished his breakfast, he said solemnly, "Don't leave the house today, my Maggie."

Maggie noted that he took a container of red paint with him when he left the house. Was he going to fight again? While she started preparation for the day's food, Maggie pondered the strange situation, but she shoved the obvious answer out of her mind until Haldonna burst into the door. The tears covering the girl's face were so unusual that Maggie dropped the pot she was holding, breaking it, and spattering the contents all over the floor.

"Today he will be killed, Maggie. Burning him at the stake."

"Burning him at the stake!" Maggie repeated, an acid froth rising in her mouth. "God," she prayed, "have I made no impact on this man at all? You said Your word wouldn't return to You without results. What can I do?"

Haldonna groveled on the floor, overcome by her sorrow. "We told our love for each other this morning when I took the gruel. I didn't know they were to be our last words."

Anger seized Maggie then, and her hands trembled as she drew Haldonna to her feet. "We're not giving up yet. I will not stand by and let this evil thing happen." She almost dragged Haldonna from the room.

"Towaye won't like," she muttered.

"And Maggie doesn't like this senseless sacrifice of life either." Breaking into a run, Maggie could hear Haldonna's feet pattering at her heels as she cleared the small forest area between her cabin and Winnetoon.

Shouts from the temple area assailed her ears before she left the trees, and in the distance, she saw the warriors capering around the sacred circle. Bodies streaked with red paint, brandishing war weapons, they were a formidable sight, and Maggie momentarily checked her speed. Was she willing to give her life for the cause of this stranger? Was her death to serve as a sacrifice of witness to the truth that Jesus had been willing to die for others?

Towaye, his body streaked with red paint, stood in the midst of the circle, towering over the prisoner, arms folded, watching with unemotional face as an old man ignited the wood heaped around the boy's feet. The shouting increased to a clamor. In her haste, Maggie had only one glimpse of Little Raven, and although fear showed in his eyes, he stood erect, bravely facing his enemies.

Racing into the circle, Maggie knocked the torch from the hand of the old man, and holding her skirt above her knees, she quickly stamped out the flames around Little Raven. Grabbed from behind in such a violent grip that her teeth chattered, Maggie was roughly turned until she stood facing Towaye, whose black eyes were venomous. Had his love turned to hate? In that moment Maggie knew her life hung in the balance. *Only a step between me and death. Who had said that?* she wondered irrationally.

Almost cowed by the hostility she sensed in the suddenly quiet circle of people, Maggie stared belligerently into his eyes. Little Raven was no longer the center of attraction, for everyone stared at Maggie and Towaye.

"Why, my Maggie? Why have you shamed me before my village? Would you leave me no respect at all?"

"Which is more important to you—your pride or your sister's happiness? Haldonna loves him. Don't you know that?"

Momentarily his gaze left her, to observe Haldonna, kneeling at the prisoner's feet. Her arms around Little Raven's legs, she looked beseechingly at Towaye.

"Haldonna is Algonquian. Should have known better than to love our enemies."

"Love comes sometimes whether one wants it or not. Please release the boy, Towaye. I know how she suffers. How do you think *I* would feel if I had to stand by and see you burned at the stake?"

A subtle change came over Towaye's face as he recognized the significance of Maggie's words, and he caught her wrist in a grip so tight that her hand was numbed. "Do you know what you have told me? But it is not enough. Say what you mean. Say you'll love me, your body for his life."

"All right, if you want to know. I love you, love you, love you." She shouted the last words at him. "But not even for the life of this prisoner will I do what you ask. I will not be your woman, so take my life. Let me die in place of this boy. If I've shamed you, take *my* life—that will restore the pride that's so important to you. I can't live like this any longer."

He released his grip so suddenly that she flung her arms wildly to retain her balance. Stepping to the prisoner, in one quick movement, he cut the bonds that secured the boy's hands and feet, and shoving the boy toward Haldonna, he said, "He's yours. His life as man of this tribe can replace our brother. Vengeance is done." With those words, he motioned the tribesmen to follow him, and Maggie was left alone in the sacred circle with Haldonna and Little Raven.

"What will Towaye do to you now? Will he beat you?" Fear for her friend showed in Haldonna's eyes.

Wearily, Maggie rose to her feet. "I really don't care."

All the next week, Towaye didn't enter Maggie's house, although he extended his protection over her. He set up camp near the edge of the clearing, and at night, she was always conscious of his protective presence nearby.

In those days Maggie learned how easy an Algonquin union was, and why it must be difficult for Towaye to understand her hesitation to become his woman. Haldonna simply accepted Little Raven as her mate, and he moved into the house of Tananda. Just as simple as that, Little Raven, once an enemy, was now accepted as one of her people. *I guess they've taught me a few things about loving my enemies*, Maggie thought ruefully.

Although they had accepted Little Raven, the Algonquians had become hostile toward Maggie again, and she sensed their enmity each time she encountered any of them. But they forgot their anger in the wake of a sickness that spread through the village.

"A baby die this morning," Haldonna reported when she met Maggie at the river where they were folding their laundry.

"Not Cauda's?" Maggie said quickly, knowing what a blow it would be to the family if their brother's child died.

"No, another baby. Strange sickness we've not had before. Red spots all over body."

In a few days many of the villagers were ill with a similar disease, including Peter Colman's woman. Maggie went to his hut, and as she observed the feverish woman on the mat, Colman said, "It's measles, ain't it?"

"I think so," Maggie admitted. "My brothers and I had the disease several years ago, and it seems the same. But it's a contagious disease. Where could this isolated tribe have gotten measles?"

"The first one to get sick wasn't from this tribe. We had a family travel past Winnetoon a few weeks ago. The man was sick when they stopped here, and they had already visited the English settlement. I've heard before that the American natives can't throw off white man's diseases."

Maggie knelt beside the woman whose breathing was forced and unnatural. Her mouth was open, and Maggie could see white spots inside her cheeks and mouth. The bronze face was speckled with red, as were her hands and the feet that moved restlessly.

"I'd help if I could. I won't take the disease again, but what cure is there for measles? What are they doing to help the sick?"

Colman picked up his son who was crawling toward his mother. "Not much. The weroance comes in once a day, sprinkles tobacco on her, goes through some kind of incantation, but you know that won't help. Every day they take the sick to a steam house for a few hours, then dip them in the river."

Maggie stood up quickly. "Why, that's the worst thing they could do for a fever! No wonder they're dying."

Colman wiped a hand across his forehead. "I'm not as brave as you, Miss Maggie, and I won't interfere with their ways." At that moment, several women came in, lifted the woman, mat and all, and carried her out of the hut. Maggie and Colman watched silently.

"Maggie," Haldonna whispered in a conspiratorial manner. "Don't tell, but Little Raven is homesick. Wants to go to his tribe for a visit, to tell his mother he's alive."

"Are you going to stay there?" Maggie inquired sharply.

"No, Little Raven is part of our tribe now in exchange for my brother, but won't tell Tananda because she might forbid us to leave. We slip away tomorrow night. The trail goes by the English settlement, Little Raven says, and we take you with us, if you not tell Towaye."

Maggie caught her breath. At last she had the opportunity she had wanted! She glanced toward Towaye's camp. If he had been his usual, considerate self, she might have had reason to stay at Winnetoon, but no words had passed between them since she had interfered in their enemy's sacrifice. He would probably be glad to get rid of her, now that she had shamed him before his people.

Slowly she nodded her head. "I'll go."

"We leave when the night is the darkest. When you hear the whistle of the nighttime bird, three times, meet us at the river."

Maggie spent a sleepless night, irritated that she should hesitate for a minute to get away. She left a candle burning, and the flame threw flickering shadows around the room as she thought of her days here—of Towaye's love and his kindness, and of the many moments she had shared with him, and the others, in her makeshift school room. But that was all in the past. She might as well leave.

The next day Maggie had little time for regret, for Haldonna came early with the news, "Peter Colman's woman die last night," and Maggie went with her to his hut. Perhaps with the tribe mourning for the woman, it would be easier for them to get away.

Haldonna thought so, too. "We come here to mourn, and we slip away before the dawn."

Colman sat in the corner of the room, holding his son, unmistakable signs of grief covering the man's face.

Maggie encountered Towaye as she returned to her home, and she looked at him keenly, her reaction to him sharpened by the impending separation. Was it her imagination, or did he look paler than usual? She wondered where he'd been eating, for he looked gaunt. She longed to speak to him, to touch him, but he brushed by her without a word.

At eventide when Maggie went to milk the goat, and to feed her chickens, she looked across the clearing, and was amazed to see Towaye rolled in his mat, bearskins covering him.

"In this weather, how can he stand that heavy bearskin?" And it wasn't like him to be sleeping in the daytime. As the shadows lengthened, she kept watching his camp, and still Towaye didn't stir. At last she could stand it no longer, and she approached his camp.

"Are you all right, Towaye?" she asked, but when no answer came, she decided that he must be sleeping. She knelt beside him, touched his face, and drew her hand back from the warmth of his skin.

"He's sick," she gasped, and cold chills almost suffocated her. "The measles! He has the measles." She looked at the overcast sky, where a few rumbles

151

of thunder in the distance, indicated approaching rain. "He can't stay out here."

She shook his shoulder, finding it warm to her touch. "Awaken, Towaye," she said, and he turned over on his back, his eyes opening partially.

"Come into the house," she said. "You're sick, and I'll care for you."

He protested at first, barely coherent, but eventually she coaxed him into the house, where she laid him on his accustomed mat near the fireplace. Remembering her mother's bathing her face often with fresh water when she had been sick with the measles, Maggie hastened to the river. She stopped at Tananda's lodge and asked for some medicine, and was given some powdered leaves of willow, sumac, and dogwood, which the older woman said was good for the fever.

Towaye was sitting up when she returned, but his eyes were glazed, and he didn't seem to know where he was. A rash was breaking out on his neck. No doubt remained—he had contracted measles. She refused to think about what had happened to Colman's wife as she stirred the herbs into a cup of water and forced Towaye to drink it. She gave him a small piece of willow bark, and encouraged him to chew it. According to Tananda, that was good for the fever also.

Maggie barely noticed the thunderstorm, pelting the cabin with heavy drops, as she worked with Towaye. When he lay back at last with some ease, Maggie took time to eat a bowl of cold gruel. She managed to put some of the gruel, mixed with goat's milk, down Towaye's throat, but he vomited the food as quickly as it touched his stomach.

"Head hurts," he mumbled over and over, and brushed away Maggie's hand when she tried to massage his forehead. He stirred often with a slight cough, and she had to continually wipe his nose.

Long after midnight, Maggie finally leaned back against the wall, hoping to get some rest. The storm had ceased, and nightbirds sang nearby. She closed her eyes, wanting to sleep before Towaye became restless again.

Maggie was drowsing in a sea of nothingness, when she was startled by a discreet tap at the door. Not wanting Towaye to rouse, Maggie hastened quietly to the door.

"Yes?" she whispered.

"Are you ready to go, Maggie? We have whistled for you many times." Haldonna's words drifted into the quiet room, broken only by Towaye's raspy breath. Maggie opened the door, and in the darkness, made out Haldonna's form.

"Oh, Haldonna, I'd forgotten all about leaving. Towaye is so sick. I've been working with him all night."

Haldonna nodded sagely. "Good time to leave then. He not follow you."

Maggie went to kneel beside him. She touched his face tenderly, her fingers outlining the parched lips.

Leave! intuition told her. *This may be your last chance to get away. If he dies, the tribe will turn on you.*

Haldonna tugged at her garments. "Hurry, Maggie. Little Raven is waiting, wants to put many miles behind us before the morning dawns."

"Where morning dawns," Maggie whispered. *Did it dawn for her in this man?* She couldn't face the fact of his death, but she squarely considered the possibility that she would no longer have him, either if she left, or if he died. *If he dies, I don't know that I want to live. The tribe can do to me what they will.*

"I won't leave him, Haldonna. Go without me." She embraced the girl, who slipped silently into the night.

By morning Towaye's condition had worsened, and he stared at her with unseeing eyes, but then a new problem arose. Hearing footsteps outside, she went to the door, where several men were standing. One of them held a long mat. "Take Towaye to steam house and river," one man said.

Maggie backed away from them. "Oh, no, you don't," she said. Running to Towaye, she jerked his knife from his belt. Standing in the doorway, the wind blowing her golden hair, the drawn knife in her hand, she must have seemed a formidable menace, for the Indians backed away.

Although she barricaded the door to keep out the intruders, she knew that she couldn't stay awake forever, and she feared if she dozed, the townsmen would carry Towaye away. His only hope of survival lay in her nursing, and she must keep him in the cabin. Lying in a steamy hut, followed by immediate immersion of the body into the cool stream, must have contributed to the death of Colman's woman, and she would have none of that for Towaye.

Maggie was worried about how much longer she could watch over him, for her supply of water was running low, but late in the afternoon of the third day of his sickness, Colman hailed her from outside the small window.

"Need any help, Miss Maggie?"

"Oh, yes, I do," Maggie breathed in thankfulness. "Will you bring some wood and water? I'm almost out of both."

For the next two days, Colman brought supplies, and sat beside Towaye while Maggie went into the clearing to care for her livestock. She tried to make tempting food for Towaye, but he refused all sustenance.

One night he sat up abruptly, clutching her to his breast. Arms that were usually strong as iron, could scarcely hold her now, she realized.

"I carry my love for you to the grave, Golden Hair." He sank back on the mat, seemingly lifeless, but Maggie wouldn't give up. She wiped his face with a moistened skin, knowing that the crisis was near.

"God, I ask for his life. And if You grant my wish, what will I do about him when he is well? His life is too important to me to be lost. And, Father, what about his eternal security? I can't bear to see him go to his grave unprepared to meet You."

Maggie didn't leave him that night, and by morning she seemed to note a difference. His brow was cool for the first time in days, and when he opened his eyes, his rationality seemed restored.

"My Maggie," he whispered, and she lay beside him on the floor, her arms around him, weeping on his shoulder, the first tears she had shed in all of that long vigil. He tried to lift his arm to embrace her, but he was too weak.

"Almost died?" he asked.

"Yes, I feared you would," she said, stroking the dark hair that seemed lifeless now. He tried to sit up, but fell backward on the mat.

"Weak like a baby."

"Yes, and you'll be like that awhile, but I'll soon have you well. Will you eat a bit of food now?"

"Water, my Maggie. Only water." But she slipped some herbs into the water, and he drank it willingly. In the next few days, Towaye gained strength as Maggie plied him with puddings made from milk and eggs. It was a great occasion for both of them when he was able to sit at the table to eat.

That day, he reached for her hand, and said, "Sorry, my Maggie, for the way I've treated you. Loved you all the time, but just a mean streak that made me stubborn. Angry at myself for I didn't want to go to war, didn't want to execute Little Raven, but forced myself because it was our way. Your way better, I know."

Maggie lifted his hand to her cheek, and looked at him with wondering eyes. *The teachings of the Bible had made an impact.*

Colman reported from the village that the epidemic had apparently halted, and the villagers felt fortunate that only five of their number had died.

One night as Towaye and Maggie sat together on the step in the gathering dusk, a late-season whippoorwill sang to its mate, and Maggie's spirit vibrated to the pathos in the bird's song. Her heart soared, and she felt a closeness to Towaye that she had never experienced before. He must have sensed it, too, for he reached for her hand.

"Now you have saved *my* life, so no more debt to me. No longer prisoner. You are free. It is our way."

No, she reasoned, *I will never be free again. You've become so much a part of my life that I'm no longer my own.* But she said nothing, and they sat in companionable silence, their shoulders touching, as the whippoorwill filled the night with its plaintive song.

CHAPTER 11

"Now THE FIRST DAY of the week, came Mary Magdalene, early when it was yet dark, unto the sepulchre, and saw the stone taken away from the tomb. Then she ran, and came to Simon Peter, and to the other disciple whom Jesus loved, and said unto them, They have taken away the Lord out of the sepulchre, and we know not where they have laid him."

Towaye was carving a bowl, the scent of fresh cedar filling the cabin, and Maggie was reading the Resurrection story to him when Peter Colman entered the cabin.

Colman listened to the reading until Maggie laid the Bible aside, then he spoke with a glance toward Towaye.

"Since my woman died, I can't be settled here at Winnetoon." His words were directed to Maggie, but he kept his eyes fastened upon Towaye. "I'm going to leave for the English settlement—take my son so he can learn the ways of my people." Towaye raised his head swiftly, and Colman looked away. "You asked me once, Miss Maggie, if I ever went to the settlement, to take you along. You could be of help to me in caring for the boy on the journey. I leave two days from now—let me know if you want to go." Colman made a hasty exit, perhaps fearing Towaye's wrath at the very suggestion.

Towaye continued to carve on the bowl, but the hands that had been carving so carefully before now cut large gashes into the wood, and finally he threw the marred bowl into the fireplace, where it thudded against the back wall.

He strode to the door, and his tall frame shut off the light from a rapidly sinking sun. Maggie hadn't moved since Colman had uttered his words, and now irrationally she thought *It isn't the land where morning dawns anymore; the sun of my life is setting.*

With his back still toward her, Towaye muttered, "Do you want to leave?"

"I don't know." Her words were almost a whisper. "Since I came to Winnetoon, I have often longed for the day when I could be with my people, see my friend, Jane Pierce, again. To be honest, I have grown accustomed to our life here, but if I don't go, I will always wonder if I should have."

He dropped to his knees beside her, and took her hand. "My Maggie, I will hold you no longer. As I have told you, you have gained your freedom by saving my life, for though I have longed for you, Golden Hair, I have given up that you will ever come to me. Many nights, as you have slept, I have stood by your bedside, while the force of my soul and body have cried out to possess you, and I have waited for you to cry out for me. I have given up that dream."

"Oh, please don't say those things! I've told you why I couldn't be what you wanted." Tears were brimming in her eyes, and her lips trembled.

"No, Golden Hair. Richard is just the excuse you have used. Even without Richard's vows, you would not have submitted to me. I am different, not of your people. You draw back from me because I am not of your blood, of your religion, not of your ways."

Maggie reached toward him, but he drew away, and would not let her touch him. He stood and walked slowly around the cabin.

"Once when I was a boy, I had two pets. One was a tiny hawk, whose foot I tied to the post. The other was a raccoon I had saved from death. I thought they belonged to me until a wise man of the village said, "No, they are not yours. Their spirits are not free. Turn them loose. If they have love for you, they will return to your lodge. If they leave the village, you will know they had never belonged to you.'"

Maggie listened breathlessly, questioning why he told the story to her now.

"I cut the cord, and the hawk flew away, and as it soared higher and higher into the sky, I thrilled at the grace of its movement. The hawk had wanted its freedom, and it did not return. But though I freed the raccoon from its pen, and even tried to drive it from the village, it refused to leave. The rest of its life, the animal stayed with me."

Maggie's soft sobs fell like peals of thunder into the quietness of the room.

"If you are like the hawk or the raccoon, I do not know, Golden Hair, but because of my love for you, I will set you free."

He slipped quietly from the cabin, and by the time he returned, Maggie was in bed, but she had not gone to sleep although the hour was late. Was he right? Had she shunned him because of his race? She, who had wanted to evangelize among his people—would she be ashamed to call him her husband?

She was sure that Towaye didn't sleep either, for he

turned often on his mat. Haggard and wan from lack of sleep, Maggie's head reeled when she sat up in bed the next morning. At her movement, Towaye stood quickly.

"Have you decided?" he asked at once, apparently impatiently awaiting her decision.

"I will go with Colman to the English village."

His face didn't reveal his thoughts, leaving Maggie to guess his feelings about the statement. His eyes scanned her face, and he slowly approached the bed, drawing his knife from his belt. When he raised the weapon toward her, Maggie shrank back against the wall, but with one deft move, he cut the long lock of hair that often hung loose over her shoulder, and with it in his hands, he left the room.

The morning sun was high by the time Maggie generated enough energy to enter Winnetoon and approach Colman's hut.

"I've decided to leave when you do."

"Will you ever come back to Winnetoon?"

Maggie kicked the loose dirt at her feet, looking at the cloud of dust it raised. "I don't know. I don't think so."

"Then you will want to take your possessions, but plan to travel light. Just pack what you can carry, for I'll be burdened with the boy. I am taking along a young man from the village to carry my clothes, and some skins I want to use for barter. He might be able to carry a few of your things."

"No, I have very little to take. I brought nothing here with me. The house is all that I can call mine, and I can't very well take it."

"We leave at break of day tomorrow." As Maggie started away, he said crisply, "How's Towaye taking this?" She shook her head, unable to answer.

Maggie listened impatiently for Towaye's step, wanting to discuss her reasons for going, but he didn't

160

return to the cabin all day. At dusk, she went to Tananda's lodge to find him, but his mother said, "Towaye go into forest."

"What should I take with me?" Maggie mumbled aloud as she moved around the cabin. She held up the feather dress and buried her face in the soft skirt, but she hung it back on the peg.

She eased her feet into the soft moccasins Towaye had given her on the first day at Winnetoon. Those she must have, and she laid them in the deerskin pack. Her Bible joined the moccasins. She wouldn't take the other books—perhaps Towaye, with the smattering of English words he'd learned to read, could make use of them.

She hung the conch-shell necklace over her head, rubbing the smooth shell against her cheek. How well she remembered the day he'd given it to her as they sat looking out over Roanoke Island. That was the first day she'd realized that his interest in her must be taken seriously.

Maggie's sighs came often as daylight waned, and the cabin became shrouded in darkness. She took one last look around the clearing before she closed the door. The grazing goats, and the hen hovering over her chickens, reminded Maggie of the sacrifices he'd made to create an English environment for her at Winnetoon.

She said aloud, "If you stay, are you willing to become his wife? You know you can't live in this cabin any longer without yielding to him. Are you prepared for that?"

With a touch of panic in her movements, she tied the thongs of the deerskin pack. *It was now or never!* She would be ready when Colman started in the morning.

Maggie slept fitfully. Morning brought the unpleasant truth that she was still alone, and opening the door, Maggie scanned the nearby woods hoping for a glimpse of him. How could she leave without telling him goodbye?

Knowing that daybreak was near, she packed some food, and fastened on her moccasins. She put on the leather breeches that Towaye had given her when Marona had destroyed her clothing.

Hearing Colman's hello on the outside, Maggie knew she could delay no longer. He wasn't coming to see her leave. Dropping to her knees beside his sleeping mat, Maggie embraced the mat as though her beloved was sleeping there. Placing her lips where his head always lay, she choked back a sob, and without looking back, she ran out the door to join Colman.

In order to have his hands free to handle his bow, and a quiver of arrows, Colman had strapped his son to his back. A young man, carrying two heavily laden packs, stood beside the Englishman.

"Ready?" Colman asked, and at Maggie's nod he started toward the river. Maggie followed at his heels, and the young man fell in behind her. She paused only once, to pat the side of the black and white nanny goat, and Winnetoon was left behind. Only its memory remained.

Six days passed—days of climbing hills, wading streams, fighting mosquitoes, and sweltering in the humid temperatures. The sun was directly overhead when Maggie looked down on the village that resembled a corner of English countryside. "Looks kinda like home, don't it?" Colman said slowly as he shifted the boy on his back.

Maggie nodded solemnly. For a moment she felt a twinge of nostalgia that could only be homesickness, unsure whether she was longing for Devon, England, or Winnetoon. Leaving Winnetoon hadn't brought the delight that she had anticipated when considering a reunion with her friends. Towaye was constantly in her thoughts. How was he enduring the empty house?

Colman reached back to pat his son, who was starting to fuss. "I didn't know this little tyke was getting so heavy until I tried carrying him for a week," he said affectionately. "Guess we might as well go on down and meet the folks," he continued somewhat reluctantly, and Maggie wondered if he, too, was having second thoughts about rejoining the English.

The settlement was larger than Winnetoon, Maggie decided, as they approached the area by descending a barren hill that gave the settlement an unobstructed view of the forest area. The houses were constructed of split laths and daub, covered with thatched roofs like the dwellings on Roanoke Island. The largest building probably served as a communal guard house where the unmarried men lived. Twelve of the buildings seemed to be private dwellings, and one small building with a cross was obviously a place of worship.

Playing at the edge of town, which fronted on a river, was a group of children, and Maggie immediately recognized one of them as the redheaded John Prat, although the boy had grown considerably in the past year. The children looked warily at the strangers, and started running toward the houses when Colman approached them.

"Wait, John," Maggie called, and the Prat child halted upon hearing a familiar voice. "I'm Maggie Lawrence. Where do your father and Aunt Jane live?"

Speechless, the boy pointed to the nearest house. Colman waited while Maggie stepped up to the closed door that opened at her knock. Jane Pierce stood in the opening, her brown eyes registering disbelief.

"Why, Maggie," she said in shocked tones. Then

she grabbed her friend by the arms, and cried, "You're alive! All these months I've believed you dead."

She looked beyond Maggie to the men in the road. "Who is this?"

"You remember Peter Colman, Jane. He was at Roanoke Island last summer."

Colman touched his hand to his forehead. "Pleased to meet you again, ma'am. If you can take care of Miss Maggie, I'll move on into the village to find shelter for my boy and myself."

Maggie had grown fond of the child during the time she had cared for him on the trail, and she said, "Do you want me to keep him until you can make some arrangements? That is, if Jane doesn't mind."

Jane hesitated momentarily, obviously noting the native blood in the child. "Of course, I don't mind." And she motioned to Colman. "Leave the child here, if you like."

Jane drew Maggie inside, and closed the door as soon as Colman left. "The house stays cooler if we keep it closed during the hottest part of the day. The wet heat is the worst part of living in this country."

"Yet you've done well from the looks of things."

"Yes, we have done well," she said, as she hurried around to make a cup of sassafras tea for Maggie. "We made it through the winter with a minimum of discomfort, and only a few deaths. The men hunted and added to our diet, and they cleared the fields, so that this spring, we could plant crops." She motioned toward the river as she placed a cup of steaming liquid in front of Maggie. "Perhaps you noticed some of our crops as you came into the village. The soil is very fertile, and we're expecting to do well."

She drew her chair close to Maggie, and took the fretting child until Maggie could drink the tea. "But enough of that. What happened to the others, Maggie?

Some of our colonists stopped at Roanoke Island last winter when they were on a hunting trip and found the place had been vacated. What happened?"

"About six weeks after the rest of you left, we were attacked by some natives. All our people were killed except me."

"How did you escape?"

"Towaye," Maggie replied, and the very mention of his name made her feel lonely. Jane must have wondered at the change in Maggie's tone, for she said evenly, "Oh, yes, he did seem to elect himself as your guardian."

"He took me to his village, and I've been there since that time. Peter Colman lived there, too, you remember, and when his Indian wife died a few weeks ago, he decided to return to the English."

"But why did you wait so long to come here? And why didn't you let us know that you were alive?"

"Towaye refused to let me leave. He said he had saved my life; therefore, I belonged to him."

"I see," Jane said slowly, with a hint of repugnance in her voice.

"No, you don't see," Maggie said bitterly. "It's not what you think at all. I have remained true to my vows to Richard, but it hasn't been easy."

Jane returned the Colman child to Maggie's arms, and passed a hand lightly over her friend's hair. "I understand now, Maggie, why you've changed so much. When I last saw you, you were a girl, but now you've become a woman. Being a woman is not always easy, as you have learned."

Wanting to change the subject, Maggie said, "Have you heard from Governor White, or from Richard?"

"No news from England at all. Of course, no one would know to look for us here, so a few weeks ago when we thought there was still a possibility that White would return this season, we sent some of our men to Roanoke to wait for him. Apparently no one has arrived yet. Surely relief will be sent for us before winter. We can survive on our own, but they don't know that in England."

That afternoon Jane guided Maggie around the little town. She was welcomed by all the settlers, and Maggie shared the colonists' pride in their accomplishments. Sir Walter Raleigh's American colony had become a reality! A common storehouse had been built to deposit the grain they hoped to harvest. A pit saw had been sunk into the ground to help fill their need for lumber, and a few men were trying their hand at erecting a grist mill to grind the grain they expected to harvest. Maggie was thrilled to see the ripening fields of full-headed rye and barley waving in the breeze. Patches of vegetables were growing around each cabin.

"We've learned to grow some of the native vegetables, as well as those from the seeds we brought with us," Jane explained.

"Have the Indians been friendly?" Maggie asked.

"Friendly enough, I guess, but I have an uneasy feeling about them." She looked at the Colman child that Maggie carried. "I hate to be afraid of a small boy like him, but I even feel strange with him around me. Weren't you afraid at Winnetoon?"

Remembering the kindness of Towaye, and Haldonna's warmth and friendliness, Maggie shook her head. "No, not afraid. Lonely sometimes, but not afraid."

Little by little Maggie shared her Winnetoon experiences with Jane, excluding only her relationship with Towaye. Jane wisely asked no questions about him.

"When I was teaching them to read and write, and when we had the program, I felt I was doing the work of a missionary. But when they tried to burn their enemy at the stake, I questioned whether we could ever change their culture. Do you think we're expecting the impossible when we want to reach them with the gospel?"

Maggie received no answer from Jane, nor when she worshipped in the small chapel. One of the colonists had accepted the responsibility for conducting prayers and religious instruction on the Sabbath in the absence of an ordained minister .

On the first day Maggie attended the services with Jane, the leader read from the Book of Mark. "He said moreover, whereunto shall we liken the kingdom of God? or with what comparison shall we compare it? It is like a grain of mustard seed, which when it is sown in the earth, is the least of all seeds that be in the earth; but after that it is sown, it groweth up, and is greatest of all herbs, and beareth great branches, so that the fowls of heaven may build under the shadow of it."

Maggie thought much about the parable. Had God sent that message especially for her? Had she already planted a small seed at Winnetoon, and would the day come when it would grow and engulf other villages around it? "God," she prayed, "give me the answer as clearly as You did when You called me to serve you in this land."

Within two weeks Colman had married one of the English women, Elizabeth Glane, who gladly accepted his child. Colman built a cottage, and seemed perfectly content in his new environment. The colonist who had been conducting religious services in the chapel read the wedding ritual, and pronounced them man and wife.

"We can make it legal whenever a clergyman shows up," Colman said, "but those words are binding enough right now."

Maggie couldn't help pondering if she would consider such a ceremony morally acceptable, but she was reminded by Jane that Colman and Elizabeth were not of their band of Believers. *Why can't I marry Towaye in such a ceremony? If Richard doesn't return this year, would I be justified in breaking my vows?* she wondered.

The harvest of the grain denoted the passage of time. Often Maggie looked southward, wondering if Governor White would return before winter. A month after her arrival at the village, which the colonists usually called Raleigh, the men returned from Roanoke Island.

"We didn't see any English ships at all. Several Spanish vessels passed up the coast, and when one pulled into the Sound, and sent soldiers ashore, we decided it was time for us to disappear. We didn't want them to suspect we had a thriving village here."

A few days later, Ananias Dare asked Maggie to conduct a school for the children during the winter months, but she hesitated, even in the knowledge she needed something to occupy her time. If she had wanted to teach English children, she could have stayed in England.

Promising Dare an answer in a few days, Maggie wandered down to the river bank where John Prat was fishing. She sat beside the boy as a hopeless state of frustration engulfed her, and the longing she experienced for Towaye was so keen that it cut into her heart like a sharp knife. She missed her house, the pine trees towering overhead, the serenity of the forest at night, but most of all, she missed Towaye. Maggie bowed her head on her knees, trying to avoid giving way to her grief, and John nudged her.

"Visitors," he said quietly.

Maggie glanced up, startled, to see a familiar figure approaching her. She hadn't realized how she hungered for copper skintones, and black eyes.

"Haldonna," she cried, rushing to embrace the girl. "Oh, I'm happy to see you. What are you doing here?"

"On our way back to Winnetoon. We visit Little Raven's tribe as I told you, and now we return to our village. We stopped to have a look at the English, and saw Peter Colman. He told me you were here."

"May I go with you to Winnetoon?" Maggie said, the words tumbling out before she stopped to consider. Her heart was vibrating in the most senseless manner at the very thought of seeing Towaye.

"Yes, Maggie. Towaye be glad. We leave in morning."

"Do you want to stay with my friends tonight?"

"No, we camp outside. Tribes to north might destroy our tribes if we appear friends to English. You meet us early in the morning, Maggie."

Jane offered no resistance to Maggie's departure. "You love him, don't you, dear?" she queried.

Maggie blushed, and answered defiantly, "Yes, I do."

"But what about Richard? You are pledged to him."

"What happens if Richard doesn't return? Must I deny my heart forever?"

"That is for you to decide, Maggie. It will take a brave woman to align herself with these people, but I've never doubted your courage, my friend."

CHAPTER 12

MAGGIE'S FEET HAD BEEN LEADEN when she had journeyed away from Winnetoon, but now she took the hills and swamps with ease, fretting at any delay. Little Raven and Haldonna were in love, and they had each other, so they dawdled along the trail. Although the return journey to Winnetoon was a day shorter than the trip she'd made with Colman, it seemed an eternity.

Well, the raccoon was returning. Would she always stay with him?

They arrived at Winnetoon in midafternoon, and leaving Little Raven and Haldonna at the river, Maggie walked through the trees to her house. Everything seemed the same, but absence had made her more perceptive, and she realized this place had truly become her home.

The chickens scratched in the dirt, scattering at her approach, but the goats ran toward her. *At least, they are pleased to see me*. Maggie pushed open the door of the cabin to see that everything was in place as she had left it, with one exception. The lock of hair that Towaye had clipped from her shoulder before she left, was tied with a thong, lying on his sleeping mat.

Maggie removed her travel-stained clothing and put on the feather dress. Unsure of her welcome, she kept busy, questioning when Towaye would come home. Probably soon, if he encountered Haldonna. She was on her knees by the fireplace, putting a container of cornpone under the ashes when she heard a sudden halt of his footsteps on the dirt floor of the cabin.

She stayed on her knees, and glanced at him pensively, her blond curls partially concealing her face. From the lack of expression in his eyes, she wasn't sure of his reaction to her return. She stood up, her back toward him, head down.

"The raccoon ran away, Towaye, but she's returned. Is she welcome?"

He reached her side in one leap and gathered her close. "My Maggie," he repeated over and over as if he could hardly believe the reality of her presence. His hands threaded the curly hair, moved over her back and shoulders, but at last he thrust her from him until he could look into her eyes.

"The raccoon is welcome. Oh, how I've missed you, Golden Hair!"

He kissed her then, and without reservation Maggie surrendered to his caresses. His lips on hers removed any doubt that they were meant for each other. The beating of their hearts made a melody heard only by themselves, and the intensity of their passion cried out for fulfillment. Maggie thought she couldn't muster the strength to put him away, but she did.

She sat at the table, and he knelt beside her, holding her hand.

"Why, my Maggie? Why did you return?"

Facing him bravely, she said, "I couldn't stay away from you. I missed our life together. I was lonely without you."

With a joyous light in his eyes, he asked, "Is it to be now, my Maggie? Are you mine at last?"

"We will wait a little longer, Towaye. In spite of what my heart tells me, it is difficult to forget the vows of the past. Give me until winter, and if Richard has not arrived by that time, would you be willing to go with me to the English settlement, where a man would read the marriage ceremony to us, and we could take our vows?"

"I will go," he said gravely. Kneeling as he was by her side, Towaye's head was slightly below her eyes. "I prayed to God that you would return, Golden Hair."

"God?" Maggie asked quickly. "Which one?"

"Why, there is only *one* God, Golden Hair! I thought you knew that," he said, the nearest he had ever been to teasing.

She clasped his head in her arms and kissed his forehead. "You really do believe that, Towaye?" she pleaded.

"I believe it. You have taught me well, and I believe in your Jesus, but that is all for now. My mind can only understand a few changes at a time. Difficult for me to change my beliefs—the practices of my forebears." He drew her again into his embrace. "Yes, Golden Hair, you have taught me well."

Even Tananda seemed happy that Maggie had returned to Winnetoon. "Towaye be happy again now," she said.

And the children! They flocked around her, and cried, "Maggie back. School soon, Maggie. More stories about Jesus."

Gathering the youngest of the group into her arms, she promised, "More school as soon as the crops are gathered, and when the cold weather is here." Towaye's eyes beamed down proudly upon her. She

172

loved children, and would like some of her own, but if
this present arrangement with Towaye continued, she
would never become a mother. Would she be content
to spend her life teaching the children of others?

The days after her return were peaceful ones. The
corn was in its final days of growth, so it needed no
care; thus Maggie and Towaye wandered through the
forest. Towaye looked for roots and bark to be used
for medicines; Maggie gathered grapes and other
fruits to dry for the winter. The idyllic days reminded
her of their adventures on Roanoke Island. Someday
she wanted to return there, and to visit Uncle
Thomas's grave. Occasionally Maggie thought of her
parents with nostalgia, hoping she might see them
again, but that part of her life seemed far away, so far
removed from her present existence. What would her
parents think if they could see her now?

Maggie walked warily around the clearing, trying to
reach the newest member of their goat family. The kid
had been born while she was away from Winnetoon,
and he was still wild. She wanted to pen up the
animal, so he wouldn't take all his mother's milk, for
she needed the milk for their own use, as well as for a
sick baby in the village. She was within a few feet of
the animal, and was reaching out to touch him when
Towaye came running toward her. The small goat
dashed away, and Maggie turned, intending to scold
Towaye for scaring the animal, but one look at his
face stopped her.

"What is it?" she said, hand at her throat.

"English coming."

"English! Richard?" she asked, her hand pulling
the deerskin garment that seemed to be choking her.
She'd never noticed before how tight the neckline
was.

Maggie diagnosed the look on Towaye's face as

stark fear. He nodded. "One of our hunters saw them coming through the forest. I go to look. It's Richard, with some Croatoan Indians."

"But how would he know to look for me here?"

"Guessed, maybe. Remember he came here with me once."

Maggie covered her face with her hands. "Oh, why did he have to come now? I'm reconciled to staying here. Why?" Towaye didn't answer. "How long before he arrives?"

"Not long. Just a short way down the trail."

Maggie walked into the cabin, the goats forgotten. Towaye followed her, but kept his distance. Would he try to prevent her going with Richard? No—whether she proved hawk or raccoon . . . Maggie sat at the table trying to compose herself, trying to pray.

Watching her betrothed as he strode rapidly across the clearing, she realized that Richard had changed very little in the past year. It might have been only yesterday that she had bidden him goodbye. But a year had brought many changes to her, and she wondered if those were apparent to him.

Richard pulled her into his arms and squeezed her gently, and comparing his clumsy embrace to Towaye's loving caresses, she drew away.

"Thank God, you're safe, Maggie. I had not hoped to find you here after I found no one at Roanoke Island. But I thought perhaps I could get information from Towaye, so I hired some Croatoan Indians to bring me here. They had told me about the move north, and that some of you had remained, but they didn't know what had happened to you."

Woodenly, Maggie answered him. "Twelve men were chosen to stay behind on Roanoke Island until Governor White returned with the necessary supplies. Uncle Thomas was one of those chosen, and I stayed with him." Fiercely, she continued, "And why didn't

174

you return last summer? Why are you so late in coming this year?'' *If he had returned last year, my heart wouldn't be suffering this agitation now.*

"England is at war with Spain, and last year when we returned home, the Queen forbade any ship to leave port, thinking it was necessary to have every available vessel to defend our shores. The situation is still unsettled, but White kept talking of returning. When I finally realized he wasn't going to make a move to bring supplies this summer, I secretly hired a boat and crew. When we left, the Spanish Armada was grouping to attack England, and if our journey is discovered, I will no doubt be arrested upon my return. But your parents have been almost frantic, waiting for news of you.'' He caught her hands in his. "But, tell me,'' he continued, "how did you find this place? Are you the only colonist who escaped?''

Maggie sensed Towaye's presence directly behind her, and she motioned toward him. "Towaye saved me from the attackers and brought me here.''

Richard's eyes lighted as he looked at Towaye. Grasping his hand, he said, "I knew I could depend upon you to care for her.'' For the first time, Richard looked around him, noting the chickens, the goats, and the English-style cabin.

"This isn't much like the other dwellings in the village,'' he noted slowly.

"I know,'' Maggie said. "Towaye built it for me. Won't you come in?'' she invited. "I'll offer you some refreshment.''

Richard looked with interest around the small cabin as Maggie poured him a bowl of warm herbed drink and gave him some cake she had baked the day before. Seated at the table, with Towaye towering nearby, and Maggie kneeling by the fireplace, Richard looked from one to the other. Hesitantly, he asked, "Do you live here alone, Maggie?''

She waited a full minute before she answered. "No, I don't. It wouldn't be safe for me to be alone. Towaye stays here with me."

Richard pushed the food from him, and stood quickly, his brown eyes glinting angrily. He stroked his pointed beard, and recoiled from Maggie as if she had the plague. A look of revulsion crossed his face, and he stumbled backward, tangling his feet in Towaye's sleeping mat.

"And I risked my life to cross the ocean for you!"

Maggie straightened her back, and tossed her head without shame. "Wipe that look of distrust off your face," she said crossly. "Is that all the credit I get for retaining my virtue for a year while I waited for you, never knowing if you would return? I sleep there," she said, as she pointed to the bed in the corner and indicated the mat beneath Richard's feet. "And you happen to be standing on Towaye's bed. That's the closest we've slept together in this building, and even if you don't appreciate his protection, I do. Without him, my fate would have been too terrible to comprehend."

Towaye hadn't spoken a word since Richard's arrival, but now he said gravely, "That is right. She has not lost her purity."

Richard seemed embarrassed at the discussion, and he said quietly, "I'm sorry, Maggie, but you look so different in those clothes, and I noticed that you do not have my ring . . ."

"That ring was taken from me and destroyed when my clothes suffered the same fate. But tell me, Richard, why have you returned now? Are you back in Virginia to stay?"

"Oh, no," he said, "I should have explained at once. Because of the unsettled conditions between Spain and England, our congregation has decided they should not sponsor the mission at this time. I've come to take you back to England.

"We must leave today, Maggie. The captain of the ship gave me a fortnight to find you. If I haven't returned by then, he will sail back to England without me, and it is unthinkable that we miss that sailing. We will be married as soon as we reach your father's house."

Maggie looked around the room, at all the familiar objects, rugged and simple, comparing her surroundings to the regal splendor she could once again enjoy at her ancestral home. She avoided Towaye's eyes as long as she could, but one glance at his stony face told her that she would receive no help from him.

He came to her, and Maggie leaned against him, but he kept his arms by his side, would not embrace her. Lifting a hand, he ran his finger down the side of her face.

"Remember the hawk and the raccoon. *You* must decide, Golden Hair." And he left her alone with Richard.

"What is there to decide, Maggie?" Richard said sternly. "We must leave today. I have told you that."

"I must have a little time to think, Richard. For months I've looked for your return, and at last, I had decided that I would see you no more. I've become happy here."

"Happy *here*?" he said in disbelief. How pale he appeared to her after months of associating with the bronzed natives!

"Yes, happy. I've been doing the missionary work we wanted to do. Last winter I had lessons in English for the youth. I taught them Bible stories, and while I can't say I made any great impact on leading them to Christ, still I made a start. Already, I was planning for even greater things this year."

Richard caught her hand, and his grip hurt. "What is the real reason you want to stay?" he demanded.

Without flinching, she looked into his eyes. "Towaye, of course! I love him. When I left him a few weeks ago to visit the English village, the days dragged until I was back with him again. Yes, I love him. Knowing that, do you still want me to be your wife?''

''As long as you tell me that you haven't cohabited with him, I'm prepared to go ahead with our wedding.''

''I've already told you that. You can believe it or not.''

''I believe it. Now gather your things—we must start.''

''After I've waited for you a year, you can allow me at least an hour. I'm facing a decision that will affect the rest of my life. I can't make it rashly. You stay here, while I go alone for a while. I must think.''

She wandered to the river's bank, where she sat down on a rock, out of sight of the village. When she arrived there, the sun's shadow was on her feet, and she sat unmoving until the shadow had shifted a good distance from her legs.

Why did I come to Virginia in the first place? she pondered. That answer was easy—to bring God's word, and the message of Christ to the natives.

Well, she had done that to a small degree. Remembering the parable of the mustard seed, she knew she had planted some seed, for Towaye had changed a few of his beliefs. But many of the Algonquian customs would never change. If she started teaching the children today, in another generation, Christianity might spread throughout the tribes, although she would not live to see it. Had she expected the impossible?

She thought about Jesus. During His ministry on earth, not everyone who listened to Him believed His words. Should she expect better results than her Savior? What method had God devised when He wanted to change the people on earth, and encourage them to accept Him as God the Father? Why, God had sent Jesus to earth as a *human*, of course! God had become Man, so that he might identify with their problems, their ideas, their shortcomings.

Only one who is willing to become an Algonquian can be an effective witness. As Towaye's "woman," she would no longer be an outsider. *If I bear his sons, I could teach them to be Christians.* Could she wait that long to fulfill her missionary calling? God had, so why not Maggie Lawrence? God had been patient through the long years. His Son had come as a baby, and for thirty years God waited until that Son had grown to manhood.

The decision was made, and Maggie felt like a weight had been lifted from her back. Happiness lent wings to her feet as she hurried back to the cabin, where Richard waited on the step. The grave look on his face indicated that he anticipated her decision.

"God spoke to me again as clearly as He did when He called me to missionary service," she said breathlessly. "If I'm to spread the gospel of Christ here I must become an Algonquian myself. Richard, the minister at our betrothal ceremony said that vows could be rescinded by the mutual agreement of the couple involved. Will you release me from my vows, and marry me to Towaye before you leave? In clear conscience, I can never go to him without the sanction of my church."

"Is there no way I can dissuade you, Maggie? What can I tell your parents? They will never understand that you have chosen to marry a savage."

"If I had any type of writing material, I would send them a letter, but perhaps it will be better if you let them think I perished with Uncle Thomas. For in a way, I will have died. When I make this move, I'm turning my back on my English heritage. I will not expect Towaye to give up his mode of living, and I'm sure there will be days that I will be sorry about my decision, for I dislike many things about Winnetoon." She caught her breath as she saw Towaye walking toward them. *Is he worth the sacrifice?*

Her response to Richard answered the unspoken question. "You cannot dissuade me, Richard. I will stay."

Richard reached inside his shirt, and pulled out the chain that contained the third section of their betrothal ring. He crushed it between his hands as Towaye reached them. Maggie caught Towaye's hand, and he must have guessed her decision, for his eyes lighted with warmth and joy. In his close embrace, the rapid beat of his heart blended with her own.

Bringing a small prayerbook from his shirt pocket, Richard said, "I will marry you, but the ceremony must be brief. Where shall we stand?"

"The cabin will be our home, so why not there?" Maggie said, and she moved inside, her hand still secure in Towaye's firm grasp. A nerve ticking in his palm was the only indication that he was emotionally aware of the sacredness of the moment as he listened intently to Richard's words.

"Our Savior put His seal of approval upon marriage when He attended the wedding at Cana in Galilee. But from the beginning, the Scriptures have said that "Have ye not read, that he which made them at the beginning, made them male and female, and said for this cause shall a man leave father and mother, and cleave unto his wife, and they twain shall be one flesh? Wherefore they are no more twain, but one flesh. Let not man therefore put asunder that, which God hath coupled together.'

"The fact that you have left your family, Towaye, to build this residence for Maggie has indicated that you will live for her alone." Towaye nodded, his fingers closing more tightly over Maggie's hand.

To Maggie, Richard said, "In the book of Ruth, we read the words, 'Intreat me not to leave thee, nor to depart from thee: for whither thou goest, I will go; and where thou dwellest, I will dwell; thy people shall be my people, and thy God my God.' Although those words were spoken by a woman to a woman, it's fitting that we should mention them here. Maggie, you are renouncing everything for the love of this man, and for the salvation of his people. May God bless you both."

Richard read the vows, and received their responses, then he raised his hand, and in blessing pronounced, "I now declare by the power vested in me by our church organization, that you are husband and wife together. What God has joined together, man shall not separate."

"What is the date, Richard?" Maggie asked. "Someday when I have pen and ink, I would like to inscribe the information in my Bible."

"It is October 7, 1588." Richard bent forward to kiss Maggie lightly on the cheek, and grasped Towaye's hand in a powerful grip. Maggie wished she hadn't seen the tears glinting in Richard's eyes, but she had. However, she would allow nothing to spoil this moment, so she stood with a smile on her face, leaning on her husband as she watched Richard leave her life.

She would never admit to anyone that a lump rose in her throat, and that sadness gnawed at her heart when she saw him pass from sight. She had cast her lot with this new land, with Towaye, and with his people.

Almost fearfully, it seemed, Towaye touched her hand lightly. "The words that Richard said over us— have they made you willing now, my Maggie?"

Smiling away his apprehension, she said softly, "The words—they have made me willing, my Towaye."

Eagerness brought a smile to his face as he drew her into his arms.

Overhead, the pine trees shifted gently below a blue sky that was beginning to be tinted with crimson. But for Maggie, day was not ending—there, in Towaye's arms, a new day dawned.

ABOUT THE AUTHOR

IRENE BRAND, a writer for several years, has been successful with a wide variety of genre. Her first book was released July, 1984, and since that time five more of her books have been published—two program books for women, a biography of a missionary, and two contemporary inspirational romances. Mrs. Brand's visits to numerous historical sites, and a Master's Degree in History has provided the necessary background material for her newest book, WHERE MORNING DAWNS, a Serenade/Saga release. In addition to books, Mrs. Brand's works include devotional literature, religious drama, and historical, general, and religious articles. She teaches French and American History at a junior high school, and she is active in her local church. She lives with her husband, Rod, near Point Pleasant, West Virginia.

A Letter to Our Readers

Dear Reader:

Welcome to the world of Serenade Books—a series designed to bring you the most beautiful love stories in the world of inspirational romance. They will uplift you, encourage you, and provide hours of wholesome entertainment, so thousands of readers have testified. In order that we might better contribute to your reading enjoyment, we would appreciate your taking a few minutes to respond to the following questions and return to:

> Editor, Serenade Books
> The Zondervan Publishing House
> 1415 Lake Drive, S.E.
> Grand Rapids, Michigan 49506

1. Did you enjoy reading WHERE MORNING DAWNS?

   ☐ Very much. I would like to see more books by this author!
   ☐ Moderately
   ☐ I would have enjoyed it more if _____

   _____

2. Where did you purchase this book? _____

3. What influenced your decision to purchase this book?

   ☐ Cover   ☐ Back cover copy
   ☐ Title   ☐ Friends
   ☐ Publicity   ☐ Other _____

4. What are some inspirational themes you would like to see treated in future books?

_____

5. Please indicate your age range:
   ☐ Under 18   ☐ 25–34   ☐ 46–55
   ☐ 18–24   ☐ 35–45   ☐ Over 55

6. If you are interested in receiving information about our Serenade Home Reader Service, in which you will be offered new and exciting novels on a regular basis, please give us your name and address. (This does NOT obligate you for membership.)

Name _____

Occupation _____

Address _____

City _____ State _____ Zip _____

Serenade / Saga books are inspirational romances in historical settings, designed to bring you a joyful, heart-lifting reading experience.

Serenade / Saga books available in your local book store:

Serenade / Serenata books are inspirational romances in contemporary settings, designed to bring you a joyful, heart-lifting reading experience.

Serenade / Serenata books available in your local bookstore:

Watch for other books in both the *Serenade/Saga* (historical) and *Serenade/Serenata* (contemporary) series coming soon.